Lapland Outlaw

Also by Arthur Catherall:

YOUNG AMERICA BOOK CLUB
presents

Lapland Outlaw

by
ARTHUR CATHERALL

Illustrated by Simon Jeruchim

Lothrop, Lee & Shepard Co., Inc.
New York

Contents

Lapland Outlaw

1

A Lean Year for Reindeer

For anyone but a Lapp, the scene on that snow-covered upland would have been ghostly. Far away to the north, flickering shafts of light from the aurora borealis danced from the horizon to the sky—pale shafts of pink, electric blue, and unearthly green. They lit up the stunted, moss-grown birch trees, and revealed the Sarris family's herd of reindeer digging down into the snow to find gray moss to eat.

Within ten minutes after the herd had halted, Kirsti Sarris and her daughter Anna finished erecting the framework of their conical tent, and spread over it the dark, smoke-stained covering of reindeer hides. Then the two hurriedly brushed out the loose snow inside the tent, and arranged the stones for the cooking fire.

Kirsti, a woman of about forty, lit a match to a pile of birch twigs placed within the stones, and put the big cooking pot over the flames to warm. Anna, a sturdy

9

fifteen-year-old girl, brought in snow, melted it in a pot, then began to mix dough for flat bread cakes which would be baked on the edge of the fire. Soon the fire was sending sparks leaping through the open top of the tent, and the cooking pot was bubbling furiously, filling the air with the smell of cooking reindeer meat.

Out of the eerie glimmer of the northern lights came two figures on skis, Jouni Sarris who owned the herd, and his sixteen-year-old son, Johani. Their three dogs followed them into the tent and squatted on the fringe of the fire, watching with eyes which shone like emeralds as the men stuck knives into the pot to bring out pieces of reindeer meat. No one said anything until the men—and the women, too—had each eaten about four pounds of the meat.

Kirsti had made coffee in five little brass kettles, one for each member of the family, and the fifth for old Mikkel, their herdsman. He was watching the reindeer and would come in to eat later. With her heavy Lapp knife, Kirsti broke sugar from a lump weighing about ten pounds, and passed pieces to her husband and son. They held the sugar between their teeth and drank the coffee through the sugar.

When he had finished, Jouni wiped his wooden mug with a handful of dried grass, then felt for his empty pipe. He looked at it longingly, and put it away again. "After Mikkel has eaten we shall go on," he announced. "I have not smoked my pipe for two weeks, and—"

"And so we shall all travel until we are exhausted just so you can smoke," his wife interrupted. "Not so, Jouni. Anna is tired, the herd is tired. All the other herds are behind us. We have moved faster than anyone."

10

"But I need tobacco," Jouni said disappointedly.

"I could ski ahead to the trading post and get you some," Johani volunteered. "When I tell Paavo Niklander that we will arrive tomorrow, I know he will let me have a packet of tobacco. He is always glad when the reindeer come in. It is good for trade."

"There will not be much good trade this year," Jouni grunted. "It is many years since so few calves lived through the spring. There will be no new cloth for a dress, Anna. Thirty reindeer is all we can afford to sell."

"If you want me to, I can go for the tobacco now," Johani said, trying to cheer up his father.

"No, son—your mother's right. You need to rest," Jouni said. "You can ride ahead of us into the settlement early tomorrow morning. I can wait until then."

Jouni went outside to look at his animals, and soon afterward Johani wrapped himself up in a reindeer blanket and lay down to rest. Anna stretched out to sleep, too.

Twenty minutes later old Mikkel came in, his bushy eyebrows rimmed with the first hoar frost of the night. No one knew how old Mikkel was. He could have been fifty or seventy, but his eyes gleamed with such impish fun that he always seemed to be young. He looked at Johani, who was already fast asleep.

"He is going for tobacco for Jouni early in the morning," Kirsti explained. "Men are like babies . . . always sucking a pipe."

"And I am one of them." The old man chuckled, sniffing appreciatively at the lump of reindeer meat he had hooked from the pot with the point of his knife. "Jouni shared his last shreds of tobacco with me some weeks ago. It seems months, not weeks. I shall buy extra tobacco

11

this time. A man must have some pleasures in life."

"There may not be money for tobacco," Kirsti warned. "First we must have coffee and salt, flour and sugar, and maybe some cloth. Did Jouni not tell you that this time he plans to sell only thirty reindeer?"

Mikkel nodded, and through a mouthful of steaming meat said, "It is an old saying that when the calves are few the coffee must be weak and without sugar."

When he had finished his meal, Mikkel took off his sodden *skaller*, the Lapp shoes, and laid them near the fire to dry. Then he removed the sennan grass which lined the shoes and took the place of socks, and spread it out to dry, too. Within a minute after lying down the old man was snoring.

Kirsti smiled and began to put away her cooking gear.

Mikkel slept for six hours, then Jouni came in. He wakened the old man, who drank a mug of coffee, pulled on his *skaller*, then went out to circle the herd on his skis while Jouni lay down to sleep—his first rest in over thirty hours.

Johani woke up about eight o'clock, though there was no hint of daylight. He drank coffee, ate one of the flat bread cakes his sister had baked, then went out to fasten on his skis and start for the settlement where five or six Lapp families gathered at this time of the year to sort out stray reindeer and sell their surplus animals, as well as to buy supplies for the coming winter.

The snow hissed under Johani's skis as he swooped down a long slope toward a clump of stunted birch trees. He was eager to be the first to greet the Swedish trader, for Gustav Nillson always gave a little present to the first

12

Lapp who appeared. Johani was hoping the Swede might give him one or two silver studs, for he was anxious to add more decorations to his broad leather belt.

When he finally swept down into the little valley where the huddle of buildings stood, Johani's heart leaped as he saw there were several strange sleds there—the Swede had already arrived. Since there was a light in Paavo Niklander's store, Johani hurried to the door, kicked off his skis, and dug them into the snow before going in. But he had come at the wrong time.

Gustav Nillson had arrived an hour earlier, full of plans for buying more reindeer than ever before, and had listened with deepening gloom to Paavo Niklander's tale of a disastrous spring, with far too few calves. Finally he interrupted Niklander.

"Listen, Paavo, I've heard enough of this defeatist talk. The demand for reindeer meat in Sweden has never been so great. Prices are sky-high. I want several hundred reindeer. If you can get them for me, I'll see you are well paid, handsomely paid."

Paavo Niklander spread his hands in a gesture of helplessness.

"I can't persuade these people to kill the goose which lays the golden eggs," he protested. "You forget that they live or die by the reindeer. If they sell too many now, they will be starving when spring comes round. I just couldn't . . ."

"I'll make you rich if you can get me five hundred reindeer," Gustav said. "I know you can persuade the Lapps to sell. They trust you and they'll swallow anything you say, if—" There he stopped, for the door had opened

and Johani Sarris stood outlined in the doorway, blinking uncertainly in the yellow light of the lamp.

For a moment Gustav Nillson was taken aback. Had this smiling Lapp boy heard? Gustav cursed himself for being so outspoken. If this boy went back and told the rest of the Lapps that the Swedish trader meant to try and trick them into selling more reindeer than they ought to, they might easily leave without selling a single one. There were other traders, and a trek of seventy to eighty miles was not such a great hardship for them.

"Come in, come in," the Swede roared, covering up

14

his embarrassment. He strode across the room to bring Johani nearer to the big stove.

In the lamplight Johani made a picturesque figure. His dark-blue *kofte*, or coat, glistened with minute diamonds of snow, while his leggings, bound at the tops of his boots with bright bands of cloth, were powdered white. From his belt dangled his heavy Lapp knife as well as the wooden drinking cup and wooden spoon which the Lapp always carries. Bright bands of yellow braid decorated his shoulders and sleeves, and the Four Winds cap, ornamented with four cloth spikes stuffed with cotton grass, made him look almost like a troll.

But neither the merchant nor the trader were interested in the young Lapp's dress. Paavo Niklander stared for a moment at Johani's wind-burned face, then clapped the boy on the shoulder when he recognized him.

"Ah, Johani Sarris—*bazza derivan*" (remain in peace). Johani smiled and answered the greeting.

"What about your herd?" Gustav asked anxiously. "Haven't you brought any reindeer?"

"It will be here this morning," Johani assured him. Turning to Niklander, he said, "I have come ahead for my father, Jouni Sarris. He has not smoked his pipe for two weeks. If he could have some tobacco, he will pay . . ."

Gustav Nillson did not give Paavo time to answer. "Tobacco, of course he shall have tobacco." The trader reached into a pocket and brought out a pack of the strong tobacco Lapp men loved. "Here, take him this, and matches. It is a little present from his old friend Gustav Nillson. Tell him I hope this round-up will be a very happy one, with everyone pleased at the end of it."

Johani took the tobacco, thanked him, then left the

15

house. Crossing to the window the men saw him slip his curl-toed *skaller* into the thongs of his skis and move off at a great speed toward the birch woods which were like a dark shadow on the snow-covered hillside.

"A little gift, Niklander, is bait to catch a big fish," Nillson chuckled. "The Lapps are simple people, and the boy's father will remember that I gave him tobacco when he was craving for a smoke."

"I'm warning you, Gustav," Niklander said gravely, "if you persuade them to sell more animals than they wish, it will be a bad thing for next year's trade. The smaller the herd, the fewer the calves."

"I am not worried about next year," the Swede assured him. "If I can get as much reindeer meat as I want this time, I won't come here again. I tell you, Paavo, meat prices will never be higher. And if you help me, you'll pocket enough money so that you can go south to your beloved Helsinki."

Paavo shrugged and turned away without answering. But Gustav had struck a vulnerable chord in the merchant; how he would love to make enough money to be able to leave this bleak northern country once and for all. Much as he respected the Lapps, Paavo couldn't help wondering what trickery Gustav had in mind.

2

Fire!

Later, that morning, Paavo Niklander finally heard the sound he and the Swedish trader had been waiting for—the distant *tong-tong-tong* of a lead reindeer bull's bell. The first of the herds was coming.

The two men pulled on their big fur coats, fur caps with ear muffs, and thick gloves. Outside the big wooden building they stood for a moment drawing breath through their gloved hands, to get their throats accustomed to the knife-keen bite of the cold. The northern lights, which had been illuminating the countryside for almost two hours, were now beginning to fade. It was early December, and for the next three months the sun would never rise above the horizon.

In summer there were three months when the sun never set, and each day was one of twenty-four hours of continuing daylight, often of continuous sunshine. Now night covered the land and everything was under a blanket of snow.

17

From somewhere up the birch-covered hillside, a wolf howled mournfully. "Why don't the Lapps get down to the job of killing off the wolves?" Gustav Nillson asked irritably. "If it isn't wolves that reduce their herds, it's the wolverine, killing for the love of it. I wonder sometimes if one can believe these Lapps . . ."

"Oh, you can believe them," Niklander assured him. "I have seen what a wolverine can do, and—aaaah, here they come. Stay here, I'll just go and make sure my people don't come out; reindeer are so easily scared."

He moved off to bang on the doors of the other dwellings in the little settlement to make sure no one came out until the deer were safely in the corral. Left alone, Gustav Nillson listened to the ghostly *tong-tong-tong-kolong-ong*, sounding far away, and sometimes very near, as if the snow took the ring of the bell and played tricks with it.

Finally the lead reindeer came in sight. Though it was midmorning the first gray light of day was only just beginning to brighten the sky. In that uncertain light Nillson saw the boy who had come to borrow tobacco leading the bell-deer of the herd. Quietly, with the rest of the animals following, Johani walked through the Y-shaped entrance of the corral, coaxing the suspicious bull when it wanted to turn aside.

At this time of the year, having roamed the hills for months, the reindeer were quite wild and ready to scatter at the least suspicious sound. Patience and quietness were essential if the three hundred odd reindeer of the Sarris herd were to be safely corralled. The bulls had already shed their antlers, the oxen and cows would shed theirs later. The calves born in May had small bumps where their antlers would finally grow.

18

Moving steadily and following the sound of the bell, the herd produced a strange clacking from their great splayed hoofs. Above them hung a misty white cloud; it was the breath of the reindeer, puffed out like steam into the bitterly cold air.

Standing in the center of the corral, Johani swung his bell after releasing the herd bull, and the other reindeer swirled in, beginning to move uneasily around in a circle when they discovered there was no way out.

Watching the scene, Niklander said, "In some ways, Gustav, I suppose the reindeer are like human beings; they feel safer in a crowd. That is why they will almost always follow a bell. They have come to realize that where a bell rings they will find others of the herd."

"Yes, of course," Gustav Nillson agreed. "It's the old herd instinct—to get in a ring, youngest in the middle, bulls on the outside, eh?"

They saw five more herds arrive in the next hour or so, and all were driven into the big main corral. By the time the bars were put up behind the last of the herds, well over three thousand reindeer were milling about, and the snow, which had been soft enough when the first herd went in, had become a hard-packed mass.

Outside the corral, Anna Sarris stood with her mother, waiting for the marking of the animals to begin. Turning to Kirsti, she said, "I never like ear-nicking the calves, Mother. There must be some other way."

"Ear-nicking has always been the Lapp way," Kirsti said, and with a shrug added: "It is less painful than branding with a hot iron. Anyway, you may remember you once got frostbite in an ear, and you did not feel it, did you? One has little feeling in the ear."

Anna instinctively lifted a hand to her right ear, re-

19

membering the time when she had suffered frostbite from allowing her cap to lift and not pulling it down right away. "You are probably right, Mother," she agreed, "but I still do not like it. The calves are only babies. And they squeal so."

"They squeal, but they soon forget it," Kirsti assured her. "God gave animals short memories—which is a good thing. Now . . . get ready, they are starting."

Swinging lassos, the men and boys of the six Lapp families moved into the corral and began to lasso animals bearing the ear-clips of their own herd. They swung the loops with unerring skill, and after each animal's ears had been checked to make sure there had been no mistake, it was hustled away to a smaller corral where the beasts of that particular family were being gathered.

The cows with calves were held for a minute or so while the calf had the family ear-nicks cut, so that no one else could claim it.

"I can never understand why some Lapps lasso the reindeer about the antlers while others lasso the feet," Nillson said. "Is there any special reason?"

"That's how you can tell a hill Lapp from a forest Lapp," Niklander told him. "The forest Lapp swings his lasso low because he often works in a birch wood, and if he didn't, the loop might catch on the tree branches. The hill Lapp of course is usually on a hillside, so he can swing his lasso more freely."

"Well, I'm ready for some food," Nillson finally admitted. "These fellows never seem to either tire or grow hungry."

"There are no set mealtimes—among the hill Lapps, at any rate," Niklander replied. "Maybe the womenfolk will

festoon of tiny icicles from the last time there had been a thaw. The twigs glistened in the moonlight as if they had Christmas lights on them.

Johani hurried over to the bathhouse, a timber shed divided into two rooms. In the first room were racks on which clothes could be hung to dry, and a small wood-fired stove in the center of the floor gave off a pleasant warmth. Johani stripped, hanging his reindeer-skin leggings which reached to his thighs over a rack and his *kofte* beside them.

Opening the door leading into the bathhouse proper, Johani flinched at the heat which enveloped him. Outside the temperature was a degree or two below freezing. In the drying room it was pleasantly warm, but the heat from the bathhouse showed on the thermometer as 149° Fahrenheit, and water boils at 212° Fahrenheit.

There were three benches along one side of the room, the first at chair height, the next a foot or so higher, the third a foot or so higher still. Several youths belonging to the settlement were enjoying a *sauna,* or steam bath, and flicking their bare skin with switches of birch. These produced a pleasant smell, and acted like a scrubbing brush to bring out the dirt.

In one corner of the room stood a metal tank, filled to the brim with stones, and beneath the tank a fire of birch logs purred like a giant cat. As Johani was about to sit on the lowest bench, where the heat was not so intense, one of the other boys cried, "Heat it up, Sarris. The bath grows cold!"

Johani turned to where a bucket of water was standing. Taking a dipper, he ladled about a pint onto the black stones in the tank. There was a slight hiss, for the stones were so hot that the water was turned to steam in a moment.

Johani hurriedly sat down on the bottom bench, while the youths on the top bench gave delighted gasps at the wave of tremendous heat which swept through the *sauna*.

Taking a bundle of fine birch twigs, Johani began to flick his legs, then his thighs, then his chest. It brought the blood to the surface and helped rid his skin of the dirt which had accumulated since his last bath. He "birched" a neighbor's back, and then turned to have his own back done.

Perspiration poured out of him, and he moved to a higher bench where the heat was even greater. After lying there for a few minutes, he waited to move to the top bench when several of the others made ready to leave the *sauna*.

Three youngsters, their bodies glistening with beads of perspiration, slid out through the small door as quickly as possible so that only a minimum of heat would be lost. The door slammed shut again.

Johani dropped to the ground, poked fresh birch logs under the tank, and was just about to throw more water on the hot stones when there came a cry of dismay from outside.

"Hi—hi—Paavo Niklander's house is on fire!"

For a moment those left in the *sauna* did not move, thinking that this might be a joke. Then the cry was repeated, and a few moments later they heard the trio who had just left the *sauna* chattering excitedly on the other side of the wall.

Johani hurried into the drying room. On leaving a *sauna*, one dives headlong into a great pile of soft snow put just outside the door. It is better and quicker than any cold shower. The snow closes the pores of the skin at once, and after the first wild pounding of the heart has slowed down, there is a feeling of tremendous exhilaration.

Johani opened the door, took a quick look toward the wooden houses, saw the great flaming mass, then dived into the snow. He fought his way out of it after a few moments and, with his lungs gasping for breath, turned to run back inside the bathhouse to where his clothes were hanging.

He paused for a moment at the door of the drying room, fear clutching at his heart. The ground floor windows of Niklander's house were hidden by great tongues of flame which curled up the outside wall. Masses of sparks mingled with the smoke billowing upward; the snow was painted a terrifying pink. In the moment or so that he stood watching, two men stumbled out of the house, wreathed in blossoming clouds of smoke and fire.

One seemed to be half carrying the other, and when they were only a few yards from the open doorway they fell, rolling over and over in the snow, which was already beginning to melt under the great heat.

The little settlement had come to life. Men and women, and some older children, had rushed out of the other wooden houses and were standing at a distance from the doomed building. An upper window cracked with a report like a pistol shot, and as the cold night air rushed in, it seemed to bring with it the flames pouring out of the lower windows. Men were shouting, women screaming, but no one seemed to know what to do to try to quell the fire. Out in that wilderness there were no fire hydrants, and no running water, for winter had locked the river in a band of solid ice.

Johani hurried into the drying room and jostled with the others in an effort to sort out clothing and get dressed as quickly as possible. They were all gasping for breath, having just come from the bitter cold of the snow pile; but no one had time to think of drying.

There had been a number of men in Niklander's house —two, at least, had not been able to get out until their clothing had caught fire. Each youth feared that someone he loved might have been caught in that flaming inferno.

Johani did not stop to tie the bright-colored bands which normally went about his ankles. Between him and the burning building were little knots of people, and as he drew near he heard someone cry desperately: "Jouni . . . come back . . . Jouni!"

Johani's heart seemed to stop for a moment. In the minute or so he had spent dressing, the fire had grown apace. The house and store were snuff-dry inside. With the windows shattered by the heat and the double doors wide open, the cold night air had swept in like a furnace draft, fanning the flames to a terrible fury. The upstairs windows were now shattered and red with the fire inside the building.

More terrible still, however, was the sight of a familiar figure, his own father, hurrying across the melting snow toward the red-lit doorway of Niklander's house.

Johani stopped. It was worse than any nightmare. A policeman rushed forward to stop Jouni Sarris from entering the blazing house, but he was too late. For a moment Johani saw his father silhouetted against the pink-lit doorway, then he vanished into the inferno within.

3

Race for the Doctor

Johani flung himself across the snow, pushed through the people who were standing helplessly watching, and would have followed his father into the heart of the fire if the policeman, Sergeant Peaksi, had not grabbed him. Too late to stop Jouni Sarris from taking the fearful risk of going into the burning house, the sergeant was able to halt Johani.

"You . . . young . . . fool!" the sergeant panted, wrestling with Johani and finally flinging him down into the snow, where several Lapps joined to help him drag the struggling youth away.

"My father!" Johani gasped. "He has gone in there! I must help—!"

He stopped speaking abruptly as two men came out of the flame-ringed doorway. One was carrying the other, and both were on fire. They fell into the melting snow, and willing helpers rushed forward, dragged them away

from the searing heat, and rolled them again in the melting slush. Johani recognized one of the men as his father.

Kirsti Sarris had been hurrying to see what was happening when her husband fought his way out of the blazing building. She immediately joined the little group which got the two men away from the furnace heat. She did not scream or faint, though her teeth were clenched as she helped carry Jouni toward a nearby house. Tears do not come easily to Lapp women. When a husband is hurt, the wife has to be ready to take his place.

Johani would have followed them, but Sergeant Peaksi handed him over to several men of the settlement, ordering them to keep the young Lapp away until more was known of the condition of the two men.

Trembling, unable to think for the fear which gnawed at him, Johani stood and watched while the fire ate away at Niklander's house and store as if they were made of cardboard soaked in paraffin. In a minute or so the flames *were* reinforced by paraffin, for a tank in the shop, holding two hundred gallons of the highly inflammable lamp oil, burst in the heat.

With an even greater roar, flaming oil spouted everywhere, and the pine planking, much of it rich in resin, burned with greater fury. In twenty minutes the roof fell in and a great funeral pyre of sparks went racing up into the night air, to scatter far and wide on the wind.

Johani's sister Anna had tried to follow her mother into the house where Jouni Sarris and the man he had rescued lay. Gentle hands had turned her back, and now she stood with her brother, dry-eyed and fearful, waiting for news of their father.

Nearby, Sergeant Peaksi surveyed the little crowd, their worried faces stained red by the glow of the dying fire. There were half a dozen men who could do what the sergeant wanted, but he decided Johani would be best. He knew how anxious the boy would be to help, and no one would travel faster than he, when his father's life might be at stake. What was more, it would give him something to think about. There was nothing worse than standing idly by when a loved one was in danger.

The sergeant strode over to Johani and put a hand on the boy's shoulder. "There is a telephone at Jakolokta," he said. "It is fifty kilometers from here. If you can get there quickly, a doctor can be summoned—the flying doctor. Will you—?"

"Yes, yes," Johani broke in. "What should I tell them?"

"Say that Sergeant Peaksi of the Northern District of the Finnish police asks that a doctor come at once to Niklander's settlement. Two men are very seriously burned, and two others also have bad burns."

"Will my father . . . die?" Johani asked, trying to keep a tremble out of his voice.

"It depends on how quickly you can get the doctor here. So move at once."

On a good road a car could cover fifty kilometers (about thirty miles) in half an hour if there was no other traffic. There would be no other traffic between Niklander's settlement and Jakolokta, but there was neither a good road nor a fast car. In summer there was a track of sorts, which wound its way around the fringes of bogs, through birch woods, over stony hillsides, and was crossed a score of times by streams, most of them fast-running and from one to three feet deep. In winter the bogs were frozen solid, the streams were similarly frozen, and the dwarf birches thrust their tops through a crust of snow which might be one to five feet thick. There would be neither track nor sign to direct the traveler.

Johani pondered for a moment as to whether he should take the family's *pulka*, a boat-shaped sledge which has no runners, and which can be drawn by a strong reindeer at speeds up to twelve miles an hour.

He decided to go on skis. Mikkel offered to accompany him, and Anna would have come, but she was torn between a desire to do that and an equally strong desire to stay near her father and mother.

32

Johani shook his head at Mikkel. "Watch our tent, Anna, and the herd," he said. "I shall be back soon."

He sped away on his skis, stopping once after a few minutes to look back from the crest of a low hill. The glow from the blazing remains of Niklander's house and store was reflected from the low clouds which were now drifting in from the west, obscuring the moon. The glow lit up the snowy scene and made a pretty spot of color on the grim landscape. But it was not pretty in Johani's eyes. That tint of red had brought disaster to him and his family.

He did not look back again. Just three hours later he leaned against the wooden side of the post office and rest house at Jakolokta and fought for his breath. Jakolokta was situated on a hill, and Johani had come up a mile-long slope at a speed incredible for one who had covered thirty miles of snow-covered country. His only guide had been the stars; his spur, the anxiety he felt for his father.

A few minutes after hammering on the door he was sitting by the stove, while Juolfi, the man who looked after the post office and rest house, cranked the telephone handle in an effort to call the distant exchange.

The kettle on the stove began to boil. Juolfi's wife made coffee and persuaded Johani to drink some. His heart was beating almost as rapidly now as when he had made his last terrific burst of speed up the hill. He wondered if there was something wrong with this telephone by which the Outlanders—the Lapp name for the Finnish people—spoke to one another.

At long last Juolfi got a reply, then there followed explanations, and a question to Johani as to whether the fire at Niklander's house had been put out. If it had, then the helicopter would not be able to go until daylight came.

"It was burning brightly," Johani said eagerly. "It will burn for hours, I think. The roof had fallen in, and . . ."

Juolfi turned away. He talked for a minute or so more, then put the telephone back on its hook.

"The helicopter will be on its way in a few minutes, Johani," he said. "Now, drink some more coffee, then I will find you somewhere to sleep."

"Sleep!" Johani's voice betrayed his amazement at such a suggestion. "No, I must go back."

"You cannot go back tonight," Juolfi's wife said gently. "It is fifty kilometers; you will never get there. You are tired now, and—"

"I must go back," Johani insisted. "For my father I would ski twice, three times that distance." Nor could he be persuaded otherwise. He did have some food and a final drink of coffee, then went out once more.

He had been heading north for about an hour when he became conscious of a sound from the sky behind him. The sound grew louder, a strange roar, with an even stranger swishing and clacking, almost as if a reindeer were speeding through the air.

The noise was directly above Johani now, and when he looked up he stopped in amazement at the sight of lights moving through the night. The lights moved on past him and the noise began to recede. The flying doctor was on his way to Niklander's settlement.

At the settlement only a few people still remained out on the snow. They were men from the shacks, anxious to make sure that no spark from the still-burning pile of charred timbers would start a second fire among the other smaller wooden buildings.

Among the men standing about were Gustav Nillson and Paavo Niklander. The Finnish merchant looked as if he had just awakened from a terrible dream. A few hours earlier he had been a prosperous trader, owner of a fine wooden house and shop, the latter stocked almost to the roof with the things Lapp families need—sugar, coffee, salt, flour, bolts of blue cloth out of which *koftes* are made, good knives, stocks of tobacco and matches, bright new copper coffee kettles, even several hand sewing machines.

Niklander had been quite a wealthy man until a half-drunken Lapp had swung up an arm and knocked to the floor the pressure paraffin lamp. That had started the fire and the panic. Now everything that Niklander owned had vanished in that furnace of planks and joists, doors and window frames.

"If that fool Lapp hadn't struck the lamp," Gustav Nillson said, "all would still be well. It's a shame you can't claim damages from him. But you were insured against fire, of course?"

Paavo shook his head. Who would insure a wooden building up here? He had lost everything, and apart from the clothes he wore was penniless as a beggar.

"I wonder if I could help you?" the Swede murmured.

"I would pay you back every mark," Niklander said, a light of hope coming into his eyes. "The Lapps have no supplies. If I could promise them all they needed in a week or so, they would wait. I could get down to—"

"Listen," Nillson said quietly. "I told you earlier that

I had to have a lot of reindeer this time. You can help me get all I need, and I am prepared to pay you very well for your help."

"You know the Lapps won't be persuaded to sell many this year," Niklander said dejectedly. "They—"

"Look at this," Nillson interrupted, and brought out his wallet. From it he took six folded sheets of paper. They were the printed forms of sale, with a space for the names of Nillson as the buyer and for the Lapp as seller of reindeer. There was a small space for the number of reindeer involved, the price paid, and at the bottom of the sheet was a receipt.

The names of the Lapps were printed in block letters, for few of them could write, and each man had simply put a cross against his name. To ensure that there would be no cheating, Paavo Niklander acted as witness to every transaction, and added his signature, first to show that the Lapp had actually put his "mark" there instead of a signature, and then that he had received the correct amount of money.

Singling out the sales sheet dealing with Jouni Sarris, Nillson pointed with the tip of a ballpoint pen to the number of reindeer; Jouni had sold thirty of his herd.

"If I put a zero after that number, Paavo, it will show anyone who is interested that Jouni Sarris sold me three hundred head." He looked sideways at Niklander.

The Finn frowned, then shook his head slowly. "That is foolish. After all, you have only paid him the marks shown below."

"But if I also put a zero after the number of marks I paid him, then it would make the deal fair and proper, wouldn't it? Multiply the number Jouni Sarris sold me

36

by ten, multiply the amount I paid him by ten—all by adding two zeros in the right places," Nillson said.

"But you will not have paid for three hundred," Niklander protested.

"No, I shall get two hundred and seventy beasts free," Nillson said, "and if you agree to help me, I am willing to give you the price of half that number. If I handed you the money for a hundred and thirty-five reindeer, you could start a fresh business, or even go south."

"But Jouni knows he only sold you thirty," Paavo argued, "and he will have his paper in his pocket."

"Did you see his *kofte* after he came out of the house?" Nillson asked. "It was burned to nothing. Jouni will be lucky to live. If the flying doctor does not come soon, I doubt if he will. But even if he does, he will probably be away for many months in a hospital."

Paavo Niklander stared with unseeing eyes into the heart of the jumbled pile of timbers that had been his home and his shop. It was all going up in flames.

"No one will ever know," Nillson said quietly. "And you'll never get another chance like this. At the moment you're a ruined man. Say yes and you'll have enough money to build a new store—here or anywhere you like."

"It will ruin the Sarris family," Niklander said.

"Nonsense. You know how close the Lapps are. They'll rally round and either find the children work or give them reindeer from their own herds." He held out the pen. "Here. You made out the order forms in the first place while I was counting out the money. Just put a zero after the number of reindeer sold and another one after the amount of money I'm supposed to have paid over. That's all you have to do."

37

Paavo Niklander hesitated for a long time, then grabbed the paper and hastily added the two zeros.

Nillson smiled. "By that simple little action, Paavo," he said, chuckling, "you've put a lot of money in your pocket, and a lot of money in mine. There won't be any arguing. The police know you are a reliable man; you witnessed the deal, and Jouni Sarris isn't in any position to contradict either of us. Come on, let's see if we can find a good cup of coffee in one of the houses."

4

The Swindle Works

When Johani was just over half way back to Niklander's settlement he heard the strange roar in the sky again, and for the second time he saw the navigation lights of the unseen flying machine. He stood and stared upward, and as the sound began to fade away, a feeling of peace came over him. He could not be sure that the machine he had heard was actually carrying his father to the hospital, but his anxiety suddenly lessened.

He was almost light-hearted again when he came within sight of the fire. Flames still leaped up, but the mass of burning timbers was beginning to settle now. Johani went first to the family tent, and as he drew near, their four dogs greeted him with an excited hullabaloo.

Anna was already pushing the coffeepot into the edge of the fire when he crawled in through the tent flap. "It came," she said. "Mother has gone with him. The doctor says he will live, but he will have to stay away from us for a long time."

"And Mother?" Johani was suddenly conscious of a great tiredness. He had had several hard days' work, first getting the herd across the snowy slopes, and then the work in the corral. On top of all that, his hundred kilometer race had taxed even his hickory-tough muscles.

"Mother will stay with him," Anna said. "She said that you were to be master until they come back. We are to look after the herd and try not to worry."

Johani was already dragging off his wet *skaller*. Anna took them and drew out the damp sennan grass which was inside. Before she had finished smoothing out the wet *skaller* her brother was asleep. Gently she covered him with a fur robe, tucking in his feet. She stirred the fire and added one or two birch logs. If Johani was to take over their father's duties, she would have to assume their mother's. She would be the one to cook the meals, say what supplies were needed, decide when a reindeer had to be killed to replenish their meat supply, and keep not only her brother's but Mikkel's clothes repaired.

In every Lapp tent there is a place which belongs to the woman. She sits there, cooks from there, and has behind her the boxes and bags which contain the supplies. Anna felt oddly important as she continued to sit where hitherto only her mother had sat.

Gradually the fire died down as Anna's daydreams slipped into a doze. The glow grew less; logs burned through and crumbled to graying ash; finally the fire went out completely.

Outside old Mikkel was watching the corrals. No one had come to relieve him, for the excitement of the fire, then the visit of the helicopter, had made them all forget that the wolves were still hungry and the reindeer had to be guarded.

Mikkel was smoking his pipe when two men came into view in the first light of the new day. He nodded and smiled as he recognized them. They were Paavo Niklander and Gustav Nillson.

"How many animals are there in your corral, old man?" Nillson asked.

Mikkel rubbed his unshaven chin before replying, "There are three hundred and sixty, but of that number eighteen belong to me. Thirty Jouni sold to you, so that leaves—"

"What did you say?" Gustav Nillson asked, reaching into his inside pocket. "There is a mistake somewhere. We bought more than that, didn't we, Mr. Niklander?"

Niklander's face went gray for a moment as he battled with his conscience. But his conscience lost. "Three hundred, I think, was the number you paid for, Mr. Nillson."

"Three hundred!" Old Mikkel almost dropped his beloved pipe into the snow as he repeated the number. "No, no, no! Jouni Sarris would never sell so many."

By this time Nillson had brought out his papers. He riffled through them as if not sure which paper was which, then brought out the one concerning the sale of the Sarris reindeer by Johani's father.

Mikkel forgot that he had been on watch all night and that he was hungry. He led the way to the Sarris tent, and shook Johani out of a deep sleep to hear the amazing news that three hundred of the Sarris herd had been sold to Gustav Nillson.

Johani could not read; but he could recognize the earmarks of every herd roaming the Lapp country of Finland, Sweden, Norway, and even some distance across the border of Soviet Russia. He looked blankly at the paper and Nillson repeated what he had told Mikkel— that this was a contract showing that Johani's father had sold three hundred of the reindeer herd and had received the money, Paavo Niklander being there at the time to witness the transaction.

"Father would not sell so many," Johani muttered, shaking his head. "There is a mistake."

"We'd better go and see the police sergeant then," Nillson said good-humoredly. "I don't want any fuss. As a matter of fact I thought I'd drive the herd across the border into Sweden, and send them south on the Narvik–Stockholm railway." He and Niklander walked quickly from the Sarris tent.

"No Lapp would ever sell so many of his herd," Johani said to Mikkel and a stunned Anna. But now he was growing angry and a little frightened, too. He pulled on his *skaller*, drank a hasty cup of coffee, then went outside and started down the slope toward the spot where Nillson and Niklander were talking to the two policemen.

Over by the corrals the Lapps were slaughtering the reindeer sold the previous day. They were being helped by some of the settlement children, who were looking forward to enjoying the tidbits which came their way after every round-up and slaughter. There would be delicious liver and blood sausages, perhaps even a piece of reindeer steak if they were lucky. The air was alive with their happy shouts.

Johani heard nothing of it. He joined the group of four men and noted with dismay that Sergeant Peaksi was holding the paper Nillson had shown them in the Sarris tent. The sergeant frowned as he studied the agreement.

"Now, what's all this about?" he asked when Johani came to a halt a little to one side. "You say your father wouldn't sell so many reindeer, but according to this," and he waved the paper in the cold air, "he did sell three hundred, and received the money. He's put his mark here, and Mr. Niklander has witnessed it."

"My father would not sell so many. It would leave us with no herd at all," Johani said angrily. "What can anyone do who has sold his reindeer? My father is not a fool."

"Did your father tell you exactly how many reindeer he meant to sell?" Sergeant Peaksi asked.

"No! The head of a family keeps such things to himself," Johani admitted.

"Well, this contract says he sold three hundred, was paid for three hundred, and as far as I am concerned—and I represent the law—Mr. Nillson has bought three hundred of the Sarris reindeer. That is all there is to say about the matter."

Almost crying with rage, Johani moved away, and when he was out of earshot, the sergeant turned to Niklander.

"Look, Mr. Niklander, I couldn't say anything in front of the Lapp, of course, but it is rather unusual, isn't it, for a man to sell most of his herd in this way! I understand the herds are smaller than usual this year and the Lapps not too anxious to sell."

"That's so," Niklander agreed, "but Mr. Nillson has been offering higher prices than usual; it really isn't any of my business, you know. I merely witness the deals. I saw Sarris agree to sell, and I was there when the money was handed over."

Nillson interrupted, speaking in his most ingratiating tone. "Look, officer, if you think I have done wrong in buying so many of the Sarris herd, say so, and I'll scrap the contract. They can give me back my money and that will be the end of it."

Sergeant Peaksi called Johani back, but neither he nor Anna knew anything about the money. Moreover, his father's *kofte* had been so badly charred that whatever money there might have been in the inner pocket had no doubt been burned to ashes.

Johani was so insistent, however, that his father would not dream of selling so many of the herd that Sergeant Peaksi called a meeting of the other Lapps in front of the main corral. They all agreed that Mr. Nillson had been offering high prices and that he had tried to persuade them to sell more than they wished. But no one could say whether Jouni Sarris had sold three hundred of his herd, or even three.

"My father will be able to prove . . ." Johani began, when the Lapps started to disperse after answering Sergeant Peaksi's questions, but Peaksi stopped him.

"Look, Sarris, there is nothing I can do," he said firmly. "Mr. Nillson is quite willing to cancel the contract if you will return his money. He has the signed paper witnessed by Mr. Niklander. I'm sorry, but that is it."

"I won't let him have the herd," Johani shouted over his shoulder as he skied away. "I won't!"

Sergeant Peaksi started to call Johani back, then changed his mind, and instead hailed his constable. They talked together for a minute or so, then went across the yard to speak with Gustav.

"I think you would be well advised to butcher the

44

Sarris reindeer on the spot and forget this idea of driving them across to Sweden and the railway, Mr. Nillson," Peaksi said. "The boy doesn't understand this business of a contract. It is all very simple to men like you and me, but these Lapps are mostly uneducated. He feels his father just wouldn't sell the herd, and he's rather hotheaded. Might even try to drive the herd away. Could you slaughter them here?"

Nillson frowned. "I'll have to get some of the other Lapps to do it for me," he confessed. "You know the usual arrangements: the Lapps slaughter and skin their own animals. I simply buy the carcasses. You've got me worried now."

"Oh, you needn't worry, sir," the sergeant assured him. "I'll send my constable down to the corral and tell the Sarris boy, or his herdsman Mikkel, that they must stay away until after your three hundred head have been butchered."

"Thank you very much. And I'll do my best to get the butchering started early tomorrow," Nillson promised. "I certainly never thought there would be all this fuss when I handed over my money."

"It's just a boy's stubbornness, Mr. Nillson. He'll get over it." With a nod and a smile Sergeant Peaksi walked away, giving his constable instructions to go down to the Sarris corral and stand guard there until relieved.

"And that is that, Paavo," Gustav whispered to Niklander. "I told you it would be easy."

Behind one of the corrals, where no one could see them, the Swedish trader handed Niklander his share of the money.

5

Johani Strikes Back

Down in the Sarris tent Johani sat by the fire and stared past his sister Anna to the sooted blanket-wall behind her. Neither spoke, not even when Mikkel came in.

The old man looked at Anna, then at the coffeepot, and gave a little nod of approval when the girl shoved the kettle into the edge of the fire. The Sarris dogs wandered into the tent, and even they looked dejected.

Anna brought out the big coffee sack, and it hung limply in her hands. They were down to their last pound or so of coffee beans. While the water was heating, she put a handful of beans into the battered little coffee mill and ground them to a coarse grain. With the water beginning to boil she tossed the coffee into the blackened kettle, added a generous helping of salt to bring out the flavor, then reached for the reindeer belly in which their milk was kept. The milk was almost like soft cheese, but it melted fairly quickly when put into the kettle.

Anna brought out the sugar sack, and it too was almost empty. Mikkel rubbed a not too clean hand about the rim of his wooden drinking cup and held it out to be filled.

Johani filled his cup and, still staring into space, sipped. Then he dropped his right hand to feel for the forehead of his favorite dog, and started to scratch it.. The dog's tail thumped against the thin carpeting of birch twigs which covered the tent floor, and the sound seemed to break the spell which had held Johani. He turned to Anna, saying, "A man without reindeer might as well lie down and die. And what would our father and mother say when they came back if we could only show them a few reindeer when they left us with many?"

"But what can be done?" Mikkel asked, holding out his wooden cup for more coffee. "The policeman has ordered me to stay away from our reindeer, even though I told him that eighteen of the herd were mine."

"Tomorrow the Swedish butcher will claim our herd— if they are in our corral," Johani said quietly, but there was a new light in his dark eyes. "Anna, prepare meat for us. Then we shall sleep for a little, and in the night hours we will take our reindeer away. Let the Swedish butcher find us in the hills if he can."

"What about the Outlander policeman?" Anna asked. "I have heard that now and then when a man displeases them he is taken away by the policemen, and he is not seen for a long, long time. And when he does come back he is a different man. They take these men to a place . . . I forget the name . . ."

"Prison," Mikkel said.

"But that is for men who steal, or kill," Johani pointed

47

out. "Can a man steal what belongs to him? We know that no man of the Sarris family would ever sell the biggest part of his herd. There has been a mistake somewhere, so I shall take the reindeer away and look after them until my father returns. Then we shall know whether or not he sold the Swedish butcher any, or all, of our herd."

"It is going to cause a lot of trouble," Mikkel said soberly, and bringing out his pipe, he began to stuff it with tobacco.

"You are free to leave the Sarris family," Johani told him. "Go to the corral and take your own beasts. They have your ear-markings, so no one can stop you. I think you will have no trouble getting work with someone else."

Mikkel finished loading his pipe bowl and thrust a splinter of birch into the fire to light the tobacco. When he finally spoke, there was the hint of a chuckle in his voice.

"I am an old man," he said, "and it is long enough since I did anything to laugh about. Today it is winter. The sun has gone, and for many weeks it will seem as if he has forgotten the Lapp people. One day, however, he will fool us all by peeping over the crest of a hill, just for a minute, and then we shall all be glad. When the sun does return, people will meet and say: 'What do you think of the way Johani and Anna Sarris fooled the Swedish butcher?' And when I hear them I shall smile and nod and say, 'Yes, and I helped them. I was with them.' It will be good."

"Hm!" Johani reached for his fur sleeping bag, then began to drag off his wet *skaller*. As he smoothed out the reindeer-skin shoes and emptied them of the sennan grass, he said, "Mikkel, there is a saying that 'no man eats new bread until the wife has baked it.' There will be no laughing until we have got our herd away from the policeman and up into the hills. Now we must sleep. Anna, we will eat when the moon is high."

Mikkel took off his own *skaller*, laid them to dry, spread out the damp sennan grass, then eased himself into his sleeping bag. Usually he was asleep in a matter of seconds. Now, however, he rested his head on one hand and, puffing smoke into the air, watched Anna preparing reindeer meat.

Within a minute or two, steady breathing from Johani indicated that he was already asleep. Mikkel knocked out the glowing ash from his pipe and grinned as one of the dogs thrust its wet nose toward the red spot, drawing back with a little growl at the unpleasant smell. Looking across at Anna, Mikkel said softly, "Anna Sarris, when we drove the herd here your brother was a growing boy, a good herdsman."

Anna stopped cutting the meat and said, "He is still a good herdsman."

Mikkel chuckled. "He is more. He is a man. It takes more than a boy to race to Jakolokta and back in one night, and then plan to snatch a herd from under the nose of a butcher and a policeman. This Sarris calf has grown into a bull overnight."

Anna shrugged and went on preparing food, loading the pot with meat and the last of the sprouting onions.

Mikkel wriggled deeper into his sleeping bag. His best dog hunched forward until it was lying across his feet, a position both man and dog found beneficial. The dog was comfortable, and Mikkel's feet were kept warm.

Very soon the soft hiss and crackle of the fire was joined by the sound of Mikkel's snores.

Suddenly Anna thought of something her brother and old Mikkel had overlooked. She would have to attend to it at once. Spreading one or two birch logs on the fringe of the fire so that they would not burst into flames immediately, Anna put on her own *skaller,* her bright cap, and a gaily decorated blue *kofte.* She took a lasso from a wooden hook fastened to one of the birch poles which formed the skeleton of the tent and went outside.

The day was already beginning to fade, but there was intense activity all around. Lapps were busy skinning or cutting up the reindeer they had killed. Boys and girls from Niklander's little settlement were helping. Carcasses were laid out in rows on the snow to freeze, so that the meat would keep fresh for the journey to Sweden.

Anna went across to the Sarris corral. Sergeant Peaksi's constable was keeping himself warm by means of a fire in a brazier. A heap of birch logs nearby suggested that he planned to be there for some considerable time.

"You cannot come in here," the constable said.

"I must have my reindeer ox," Anna pointed out. "How are we to drive our *pulka* if we have no ox?" The constable frowned. The *pulka,* shaped like the front half of a small dinghy, is the Lapp sledge. It is drawn by one reindeer, and is used to carry the tent, poles, household goods, and food supply, and sometimes even the woman of the family as well.

Unable to persuade the constable, Anna went to see Gustav Nillson. The Swede was glad enough to agree that the reindeer ox should be taken away and that a supply of reindeer moss should be put into the corral. Anna had pointed out that even if he had bought three hundred of the herd, that left some fifty or more beasts who needed food.

Rather than risk letting Johani and Mikkel go into the corral, as Anna first suggested, to drive out those over and above the three hundred, Nillson ordered fodder to be put in for them all. There was a little smile of triumph on Anna's face when she finally entered the corral, found her big reindeer ox and, having expertly swung her lasso loop about his horns, got the policeman to help her get him outside.

She tethered the reindeer ox behind the tent, fed him on the gray-green lichen—the reindeer moss which is the staple food of these Lapland deer—then went back into the tent.

The stew simmered gently. Anna repaired a slight cut in one of the *skaller* drying by the fire, then cat-napped for several hours. When she finally awoke there was a silence lying over the area, which told her that butchering for the day had ended. She peeped out of the tent. The moon was just beginning to rise, a silvery half, dodging between patches of cloud which scudded across the starry sky.

She shook Johani and Mikkel to wakefulness; when they were eating, she told them she had arranged for the herd to feed. "They will have had time to eat their fill, chew the cud for several hours, and be ready to move," she said, and her eyes lit up as Mikkel raised his shaggy eyebrows.

"A calf grows into a bull, and a girl becomes a woman," the old herdsman said admiringly.

"There was only one guard at the corral," Anna added. "Sergeant Peaksi's constable."

"Then we're in luck," said Johani.

The full pot was emptied before the three of them were satisfied. The dogs were given some meat, and then the bones, after these had first been cracked open and the marrow sucked out.

Then they began packing. A Lapp family often moves on each day, for the reindeer cannot be halted when they are searching for moss. A Lapp housewife can pack her belongings, even to the tent, in an hour or a little more. Later in the same day she will unpack and set up the complete home again many miles from the morning's meal.

With Mikkel and Johani to help her, Anna soon had everything packed. The last glowing ashes of the fire were put out with handfuls of snow before the tent was taken down. Then, with the reindeer ox harnessed to the *pulka*, they moved off. The dogs followed like ghosts, trained so well that a word would keep them silent for hours.

On through the birch wood they went, climbing until the birch trees thinned out and were very stunted in size. Up there the moonlight seemed more silvery; the valley appeared to be in shadow, with dark patches where the reindeer corrals were, and even darker blotches on the snow to mark the wooden shacks which made up Niklander's settlement.

At the top of the fell, or mountain, Johani halted to give the panting reindeer ox a breather. "Anna, Mikkel and I are going down now for the herd," he said to his sister. "Stay here, but be ready to move off the moment you see us coming. The policeman might follow."

She gave him a quick nod and they parted. Anna sat back on the *pulka*, while Johani and Mikkel skimmed lightly to the edge of the long slope leading to the valley, then sped on like birds, their skis throwing up a fine mist of snow which seemed to hold a million minute diamonds in the bright moonlight.

In the thickest part of the birch wood Johani halted and, using his ski stick as a seat, squatted.

"When I was younger, Mikkel, you taught me how to call the birds. First the *peep-peep-peeep* of the golden plover. Do you remember?"

Mikkel nodded and smiled. "Yes. We began with that bird, then went on to the call of the hen ptarmigan." Putting his gloved hands together he puffed out his cheeks, and anyone listening could have been forgiven for thinking that it was spring, and not the beginning of winter, as the call of the mating ptarmigan rang out in the thin, cold air: *Kopek—kopek—pek—peh-e-e-e-e-eheh.*

"And the blackcock," Johani suggested.

"Yes, the blackcock," Mikkel agreed, and again his cupped hands went over his mouth, and this time the sound was the sharp *shoooeee . . . shiooeee . . . shioeee!* of the blackcock, newly returned from its winter stay in Britain.

"It is the call of the hungry wolf I want to hear now," Johani said. "Can you still do that as well as in the earlier years?"

"A man may grow so old that his legs become stiff and his eyes less keen," Mikkel growled, "but such things as calls do not depend on youthful muscles. See if I have lost my skill."

He settled himself into a crouching position, lifted his

head as does a dog baying to the moon, and from his dark, corded throat came the terrible, keening call of the half-starved wolf—the call that sends the reindeer closer to the herd leader's bell; the call that brings the watching herdsman to his feet and makes the dogs grow green-eyed, with hackles raised and a growl growing in the throat.

Johani had been watching the three dogs they had brought down with them—the fourth, a mere puppy, had been left with Anna. At the first blood-chilling howl the dogs had risen from the snow as if plucked by wires. The fur on their necks had lifted, their eyes had gone emerald. They looked anxiously about, beyond Mikkel, and there was no doubt that the call was real enough.

"If you can deceive dogs," Johani chuckled, "then you can deceive a policeman, which is what we are going to do," and he outlined his plan of action. The old man listened, nodding gravely to show he understood. When Johani had finished, Mikkel said quietly, "Every police-man's hand will be against us. One may strike an enemy, and if the blow is hard enough that man may not come near again, afraid of being hurt even more. But if one strikes a policeman, then every policeman is our enemy. It is like dipping a bucket in a river. One takes out water, but there is no hole: much more water has rushed in where the bucket has been."

"You need come no farther," Johani said, disappointed. "After all, you are not one of the Sarris family."

"I am coming," Mikkel insisted. "I am a Sarris herds-man, and if the Sarris reindeer are butchered, then there is no need for a herdsman. I am merely telling you the danger."

"It is better not to stop and think," Johani said, rising.

"The man who stays to think whether there is danger soon sees even more danger than there is."

They skied down through the birch wood and, coming out beyond the corrals, paused for a moment to decide exactly where they should go. The three dogs were to move with Mikkel, for he had trained them from their puppy days. A word from him and they would remain silent no matter what happened.

At the back of the corrals they found suitable places: Mikkel at a spot where the corral walls turned sharply from the back into a side, Johani at the other corner. A number of small birch trees were scattered about, and these, their branches weighed down with frozen snow, gave good cover.

When he was ready, a coiled lasso in his gloved hands, Johani gave the agreed signal, the piping call of the golden plover—*peep-peep-peeep-peeep!* Within seconds Mikkel broke the brooding silence which had lain over the snow-covered valley with the high-pitched howl of a hungry wolf: *Aaaaa-owwwwwoeeeeee . . . aaaawwow-ow-ow . . . oooo. Aaaaoww-wowow-eee-eee-oooo!*

The effect on the reindeer in the various family corrals was immediate. Until Mikkel's blood-chilling wolf call shattered the quiet of the night, most of the animals had been resting, either lying in the snow or standing with heads drooping. At the first note there was an immediate scuffling as the reindeer lying down got to their feet. The slack-muscled stance of the others changed just as quickly.

Even before the faint echoes of the call, passing back and forth across the valley, had died away, there was a *clack-clackety-clack* of hoofs as the reindeer began to struggle in the corrals to get into the middle. The unlucky ones left on the outside turned to stand alert, eyes wide, spurts of breath jerking out of their nostrils and hanging like little clouds of steam in the cold air.

Mikkel called again, and at once there was an angry shout from the front of the corral where the guard had been keeping warm by his fire. Johani watched, tense. The clack of hoofs from the corral would make it impossible for him to hear whether the guard was coming around, and the moonlight was deceptive. He would have to be both quick and skillful if they were to succeed.

The reindeer were snorting now, for that second howl had cut off short, sure sign that the wolf was near its intended victim. The bulls were plunging uneasily, for they had shed their antlers in October and had only their splayed hoofs as weapons. The oxen had their antlers, but they lacked the spirit of the bulls. The cows would not shed their antlers until May, after the calves were born, and they were pressed into the center of each herd.

There was another shout from the guard as he came running along the side of the corral. Often it only needed a shout to scare away a single wolf, but if a man could get in a shot at the killer, there was always the chance that luck would fly with the bullet and bring the wolf down.

Johani saw the guard as a shadow, moving quickly along the outside of the corral. He crouched, holding his breath, trying to keep his right arm muscles loose. The moonlight brightened for a moment or so as a thin film of clouds passed beyond it. The guard came scurrying through the foot-deep snow, a rifle in his hands. As he passed, Johani swung his lasso.

The loops made a faint swishing sound as they cleft

the air. The guard must have heard it, for he half turned
his head, but the loop had settled beautifully over his
shoulders even as a startled look crossed his face.

The rifle dropped from the guard's gloved hands. He
gave a yelp of mixed astonishment and anger, then was
on his back and being dragged through the snow. At the
same moment Johani was giving once more the call of
the golden plover to bring Mikkel to his side.

With three excited but silent dogs at his heels, Mikkel
skied over and dropped a snow-wet glove across the
guard's mouth, effectively gagging him. Not until Mikkel

and Johani had tied the man's hands, then turned two taut loops about his ankles, did they realize that their prisoner was Sergeant Peaksi. He had relieved the constable who had been on duty earlier. Mikkel's eyes went round as saucers, but for Johani there was no turning back.

The sergeant was wearing a fine three-quarter length fur coat with a high collar to protect his neck, the back of his head, and his ears. It was a collar large enough to come around his cheeks and protect nose, mouth, and chin. Johani had never gagged a man before, but he did it effectively now. Whipping that warm fur collar around Sergeant Peaksi's face, he fastened it across the mouth with a piece of thonging.

"If you do not keep quiet, we shall tie it much tighter," Johani said as Peaksi began to mutter threats.

They hustled their prisoner around to the blazing fire, which was circled by a black patch of earth where the heat had melted the snow. After they sat the sergeant on the pile of birch logs, Mikkel went back around the outside of the corral with the dogs, while Johani felt inside his *kofte* for the reindeer bell he had brought along. The clapper was muffled with a piece of fur. Johani removed the fur, then threw down the bars at the corral gate.

Again on the night air came the *peep-peeeep-peeeep-peeeep* of Lapland's golden plover. Mikkel heard it and slipped through the back of the corral. His three dogs followed him, and they began to urge the uneasy reindeer toward the gateway.

Johani went into the corral. The nearest reindeer were afraid of the fire, their eyes bulging and reflecting the red light. Johani began to ring his bell. Catching a two-year-old cow by the antlers, he started to urge her out into the open.

Kong-kong-kolong-ong-ong-ong! The bell was steady, the calm, peaceful tolling which is usually a signal that a herd is moving quietly and calmly along.

The sound did much to soothe the near panic which had beset the reindeer when Mikkel's wolf howls had broken the stillness of the moonlit night. *Clack-clack-clackety-clack!* The hoofs began their rhythmic sound as the herd, bunched and still uneasy, started to move out of the corral.

Johani led the way, increasing his speed from a slow, dignified walk to a brisker movement. When they had gone two hundred yards, and were heading in the right direction, he turned and, looking for one of the larger bulls, let the first few reindeer pass him; then he tied his bell round the bull's neck.

For a moment or so it seemed as if the leading reindeer were going to halt, now that Johani was not walking ahead of them. But after a moment the bull with the bell moved on, and the *clack-clack-clackety-clack* of the hoofs grew more rhythmic again.

Waiting until the last of the reindeer were moving past, ears thrown back, breath spurting into the air, Johani called to Mikkel: "Keep them moving. I left my skis by the corral gate, and I must go back to free the policeman."

"To free him?" Mikkel spluttered. "But he will—"

"I know, I know," Johani agreed. "But we cannot leave him sitting there. The fire will last an hour; after that, unless he is found, he will have frostbite. I shall loose his ankle thongs."

Mikkel merely shrugged. To him it seemed like trapping a hungry bear and then deciding to set it free.

When Johani reached the sergeant he was greeted with an angry, if muffled, "You shall pay for this, boy. It will be prison for the rest of your life. Unfasten these thongs, and then bring back the herd. I am warning you . . ."

"I could drag you out into the snow and leave you there," Johani told him, bending down to start jerking at the ankle thongs. "If I did that, you would be frostbitten so badly that . . ." He did not finish the threat. The ankle thong had come loose, and he stood up.

"I have been kind to you, Mr. Policeman," he said, breathing hard. "Could you not be kind to me? I am not stealing reindeer. They are my father's herd."

Sergeant Peaksi was not in the mood to listen to any pleadings. His dignity had been more than ruffled by the handling he had endured. To be lassoed like some stupid reindeer, dragged through the snow, then both gagged and tied up, was more than a sergeant of the Finnish police should be asked to endure. He checked his anger and kept a silent tongue, however, in case this impertinent Lapp changed his mind and re-bound him.

"I am going," Johani said, slipping his curl-toed *skaller* into the ski thongs. "If you try to follow us, you will waste time. *Bazza derivan.*"

It was the traditional Lapp wish at parting, and Johani waited for a moment, half hoping that Sergeant Peaksi would say "*Mana derivan*" (Go in peace), but the sergeant remained silent. Johani shrugged, then gave the sergeant a gentle push.

Behind Peaksi was the little pile of birch logs; if the thongs had been completely off his ankles, the sergeant would have been able to step over the loops and keep his feet. As it was, he stumbled and then sprawled backward, his feet waving in the air.

"I am sorry," Johani murmured as he turned and sped away, "but if he is to be so angry with us, then every little time we can gain will count. It may take him a few moments to get to his feet again."

In ten minutes Johani had caught up to the herd, which was moving well through the thinning birch wood. In those ten minutes Sergeant Peaksi had shuffled his feet until the loose bonds had dropped off, and then he ran as hard as he could for the cluster of buildings up the slope. His hands were still tied, and there was no point in trying to shout, for the fur collar, still about his face and secured across his mouth, made even talking difficult.

The sergeant stood a foot away from the door of the house where Gustav Nillson was sleeping, and kicked. He continued kicking until there was a muffled complaint from within. A bad-tempered query followed, then the door was opened, just as Peaksi kicked again. A Finn employed by Paavo Niklander gave a yelp of pain as the sergeant's boot hit him in the shins. But a minute later the alarm was being raised.

Lights streamed out through windows onto the snow, and sleepy Lapps were dragged to wakefulness from where they had been lying on the floor, a dozen or more to a room.

Sergeant Peaksi was in a furious temper, and ordered every adult Lapp to get out his skis and bring along his dogs.

Paavo Niklander tried to soothe him. "If they have

gone over the fell, sergeant, there is nothing to worry about. There is only one way to go beyond the fell, and that is down the Narrow Valley. Only one animal at a time can go down the Narrow Valley in winter, and it is slow work. We shall catch them easily."

6

Will the Bridge Hold?

On the fell top, a thousand feet above the valley, Anna Sarris waited with a patience normal to Lapps anywhere. Her sturdy reindeer ox had been taken out of the *pulka* harness, and was content to rest. He showed the first signs of excitement when, despite the breeze blowing from the north, there came the faint sounds of the herd bell—a muted *tong-tong-tong-a-long*.

Anna fastened on the harness again and as the sound of the bell grew clearer and louder, held her impatient beast tightly. Soon the first of the herd were in view, looking like phantoms in the moonlight. Their clacking hoofs kicked up fine particles of frozen snow, and many of them were white up to the neck from it.

Mikkel showed up first, and there was an impish chuckle in his voice as he called out, "Ride fast, Anna —or it will be your last ride!" Then he was gone in a cloud of fine, powdery snow.

When Johani came by he lifted an arm in greeting and yelled, "Keep up with the herd, Anna, we can't manage without you."

As the last of the herd passed her, Anna gave her ox his head and flung herself expertly onto the *pulka* as it shot forward. Laden with tent, poles, pots, and sleeping bags, as well as many other small articles, the *pulka* swayed madly in the first rush. Anna dropped a foot on each side, throwing up a cloud of snow as she steadied her baggage carrier, and then they were racing after the herd.

Far to the north the sky suddenly brightened as if a fire had broken out. Banners of pale pink and vivid white began to unfurl into the sky. A few stray clouds overhead were lit by the first fingers of the northern lights and glowed as if aflame.

The brilliance of the lights seemed to dim even the cold light of the moon and as the great streamers of color spread across the sky, the snow took on suggestions of pastel shades, pink, palest green, then vivid white again.

This fell was one of the long mounds which run due north and south across Lapland, rising to a height of almost fifteen hundred feet. It was the regular route for Lapps with herds on their way to or from Paavo Niklander's store. Any other route involved a steep rocky climb out of the settlement valley, impossible for reindeer to manage, and extremely difficult even for man.

In an hour they had covered some nine miles and were on a slight downward slope. But looming ahead in the shadows was another steep slope—the great glacier which not even the fiercest summer sun ever melted.

Mikkel, sliding effortlessly on his skis on one side of the herd, dropped back as they began to go downhill a little. He swung around past Anna on her *pulka,* and reaching Johani said, "I will go down the Narrow Valley first, and I'll take a bell. The herd will not be so—"

"We cannot go down the Narrow Valley now," Johani interrupted. "Have you not looked back?"

"Looked back?" Mikkel muttered, and turned to stare at the vast expanse of snow behind them. In the light from the sky the tracks made by the herd were plain to see, an odd pattern of shadows, with unruffled white on either side where no man or animal had broken the surface.

Mikkel's eyes were still as keen as a young man's. Far away, perhaps two miles back, were minute dots on the snow. Only a man who had lived his life looking over great distances could have picked out those moving spots. Mikkel saw them and frowned. They were men; probably men and dogs.

"So that is it, Johani," he muttered disconsolately. "I knew it was a mistake to set the policeman free. The herd can go down only one at a time, and slowly at that. They will catch us before Anna even starts down the valley."

"That is why I said we cannot go down that way." Johani lifted his ski stick and pointed straight ahead to the rising mound whose face was in shadow. "We must go straight on."

Mikkel said nothing, but swinging around the back of the herd, he took up his position on the other side. The way to the Narrow Valley was on that side, and when the reindeer reached the spot where normally they would have turned right, down a cleft which looked as if it might have been made by some giant's axe, Mikkel was there to keep them moving past.

Anna drove her *pulka* over to where he stood as the last of the reindeer loped by.

"Where are we going?" she asked, wiping powdered snow from her face.

"Across the ice!" Mikkel said, and shrugged as if to indicate that it was not his idea.

Several minutes later the herd was climbing past the snout of the great glacier, and Anna came up to her brother.

"What are you doing?" she demanded, stepping off her *pulka* and beginning to lead her laboring reindeer ox. "Have you forgotten the great crack in the ice? The herd will just be swallowed up, and us as well."

The great crack, as the Lapps called the crevasse, occurred at the point where the age-old glacier turned over a ledge of rock, and split in the turning. The glacier was some hundreds of feet thick, and every few years the crevasse itself would change. As the mass of ice moved on over the edge of an unseen cliff below, the great fissure would close, but a new one would open a few yards behind it.

There were always a few snow bridges across the crevasse, which was some twenty feet wide at its narrowest point. In the depths of winter these natural bridges were sometimes crossed by men, and occasionally even by a man on a reindeer-drawn *pulka*. By that time of year the continuous hard frosts had made the bridges as hard, and almost as strong, as iron.

"We must cross the great crack or lose the herd," Johani announced. "There are police behind, and if we go down the Narrow Valley—well, you know how quickly a man can travel through it on skis. But reindeer must go down it slowly."

66

The herd was swinging to the left now, taking the only possible way up to the glacier. It moved at a slow pace and left behind a mist of frozen breath which stayed in the air like a miniature fog.

Several times Johani looked back. Their pursuers were gaining, but they too would lose time when they came up this way.

When they were near the top and were turning to the right to come onto the glacier, Mikkel swung up to cry, "Anna need not cross the great crack, Johani. She has done nothing to offend the policeman, and the Outlanders would not send her south."

Anna turned and shook her head. "If Johani goes across, I go, too. He is right. Either we keep the Sarris reindeer or lose everything in the ice. What is there for us if the policemen take the herd? For the reindeer there is slaughter, and for us—south to this place they call prison. Besides, we must do this for our father's sake. The herd is his."

Within a minute of reaching the first curve of the glacier snout, the herd was brought to a halt. Ahead of them was the ominous-looking crevasse, its depths blue and shading to a grim black farther down.

Leaving Anna with her *pulka* to control the dogs which were circling the herd, now panting and glad enough to rest, Johani and Mikkel went, one to the west and one to the east, looking for a snow bridge over which the herd could pass.

There were a number, but far too slender-looking for even a man to risk crossing. Then came a shout from Mikkel. He had found a bridge, and the herd was turned in his direction. Johani raced along to see what the bridge was like.

In places it was four to five feet wide, but in the center it narrowed to only a yard. There was snow on top of it, and the ice beneath had long icicles dangling, beautiful to look at in the mingled light of moon and aurora borealis. The icicles reflected like long diamonds, but they winked when Johani stepped onto the bridge, proof that even his weight had caused it to vibrate a little.

Fastening his lasso about his waist, Johani secured the free end to Anna's *pulka*. "I am going to walk across, Anna. If the bridge breaks, pull me up by making your reindeer ox move away from the great crack."

Anna wanted to ask Johani not to cross. She had a terrible vision of the bridge shattering under him and hurtling down into the black depths. If that happened, and if the lasso broke . . . She couldn't keep from shuddering at the thought. Yet she managed to nod to Johani. He was the head of the family while their father and mother were away.

Removing his skis, Johani moved steadily onto the bridge. An icicle snapped with a metallic *ping* and fell, looking for a moment like a shooting star until it passed out of the moonlight and was lost to sight below.

Even Johani halted at that, but after a moment or so he went cautiously on. No more icicles snapped off. He reached the center of the bridge and, to his sister's horror, raised a foot and stamped. The icicles winked in the moonlight. Anna closed her eyes. Johani walked on until he reached the far side, then he started to return.

He was back before Anna dared to look again. Then he took the reindeer leash from her shaking hands.

"I'll lead the *pulka* over," he said quietly, "and if the bridge bears the weight of me, the reindeer ox, and the *pulka* it will carry the others." He held out the free end

of his lasso to Mikkel. "You and Anna take this; if the bridge breaks, you can save me." He was not smiling; there was no suggestion of a chuckle in his voice. He was going to take a tremendous risk, and he knew it might end in death.

Tense, hardly daring to breathe, Anna watched while her brother led the reindeer across the ice bridge. He had to walk backward, for there was not room for him to walk alongside the animal.

After a minute, which seemed almost like an hour to Anna, he reached the far side. The reindeer ox was impatient to be heading upward again, so Johani turned the *pulka* on its side, then recrossed the bridge.

"Shall I come over with you?" he asked, smiling at Anna.

She shook her head and marched resolutely across. Then Mikkel, dragging the bull wearing the herd bell, went over, swinging the bull's head as best he could so that the bell tolled its heavy, not very musical *tong-tong-tong-kolong*.

Hesitantly first one then another of the nearest reindeer began to cross. Leaving the herd, Johani raced back a hundred yards or so along the trail they had traveled, and gave a grunt of alarm when he saw how near their pursuers were.

He returned at once to the lip of the crevasse, but he could not hurry the reindeer. If too many got on the bridge at one time, it would surely collapse. Casting a practiced eye over them, he estimated a hundred and fifty still to go. They were moving steadily enough, treading the snow on the bridge into a firm path. None of them seemed to be afraid.

"If they knew what might happen," Johani muttered, and shook his head. That was one thing about reindeer. They did what the others did. Each spring the whole herd made for the north, the cows because they had been born in a certain valley and wanted their calves to be born there, the bulls because they wanted to get away from the lowlands where the flies would torment them, burrow holes in their hides, and lay eggs there. In autumn the herd would turn south, knowing that there would be better feeding and some shelter from the screaming blizzards, even if there were more four-legged enemies there.

Now they were crossing the dangerous ice bridge

because Mikkel had coaxed the bull with the bell across. That bell spelled safety for the herd. That there was death on either side of them if they took a false step was something only men thought of.

Johani's heart was beating rapidly as he watched the animals. The average weight of a reindeer is about two hundred and twenty pounds, and there were never less than seven animals on the bridge at one time—over half a ton of living things. Johani knew nothing about what happens to a bridge if a lot of men marching in time cross it. Luckily for him, and the herd, the reindeer broke step.

In the changing light from the aurora borealis—pink, yellow, pale green, light blue, brilliant white—it did seem as if the bridge was actually springing up and down, and there must have been some movement, for a bull missed its step and dropped to one knee. The animal behind it tried to leap over it, and Johani closed his eyes as a yearling reindeer went down into the blackness of the crevasse.

There was hardly a sigh from below. Without realizing it, Johani had been holding his breath from the moment the bull stumbled to the time when, as if completely unshaken by its narrow escape, it trotted quietly on and safely to the far side.

A yell from behind him made Johani turn. The police and the Lapps with them were now less than fifty yards distant, so close that even in the mixture of lights, changing every moment, he could make out Sergeant Peaksi, Paavo Niklander, and a panting Gustav Nillson.

Johani did not hesitate. He stepped ahead of a reindeer cow as it was about to move onto the ice bridge and,

71

with his hands on the white hind quarters of another cow, went trotting across the ice.

Only then did he realize how much the ice bridge was shaking under its living load. It was moving with frightening elasticity, up and down, up and down, so that each second of that short crossing seemed an eternity.

"They're coming," Mikkel called even as Johani was stepping off the bridge.

Sergeant Peaksi did not lack courage. Ordering his Lapp helpers to prevent the last dozen reindeer from crossing, he stepped boldly onto the ice bridge, following a reindeer cow as Johani had done. He held his revolver up so that it could easily be seen. A minute more and he would be across.

Johani was trembling a little but he did not hesitate. As a reindeer cow stepped off the ice bridge he stepped onto it, barring the way of a bull. The bull grunted and, lowering its head, butted him. He had to give ground, but the next animal was a this-year's calf, with its mother behind it. Johani allowed the bull to reach the safety of solid ice, then stopped the calf.

The cow behind lowed, a plea to be allowed to move, for there were two other animals behind her, trying to press on—and behind them was Sergeant Peaksi.

"Get out of the way," Peaksi roared. "Get back or I'll shoot."

Johani's answer was to bend down. If the sergeant shot, he would have to kill three adult reindeer and a calf before he could hit the young Lapp.

"Sarris, get off the bridge," Peaksi yelled angrily. "If this bridge breaks while I am on it, you will be responsible for my death."

Johani looked back to where Mikkel and Anna were standing in horrified silence. They could see past the sergeant to the men on the other side. In addition to Paavo Niklander and Gustav Nillson there were ten Lapps, men with whom they were on the friendliest of terms. Yet they had been forced to come up here at the orders of the police. Standing behind them, and not looking very happy, was Peaksi's constable. He had been on Lapp duty for only six months, and was not enjoying this adventure.

"If you do not get off the bridge, Sarris," Sergeant Peaksi shouted, "I shall shoot my way over. There are only four reindeer between me and you. Now, are you moving?"

Johani looked back to Mikkel and made a motion with his hands; he was calling for an axe. Mikkel stared, frowning, but Anna, her nerves almost at breaking point, suddenly realized what her brother's gestures meant.

At first glance a laden *pulka* looks like a chaotic jumble of things covered with fur *peskes,* or robes, but to the Lapp woman or girl who has to pack it in the morning and unpack it in the evening, perhaps in total darkness, it is essential that each thing shall have its proper place. Out of that seeming confusion of objects on the *pulka* Anna produced a hand axe in a matter of seconds.

As she darted across with it to her brother, Sergeant Peaksi took the first pressure on his revolver trigger. He had meant to shoot over the reindeer in the hope of frightening Johani away, thus clearing a path for the restless animals and so for himself. But at the very last moment his nerve failed him. A shot might easily cause the

73

reindeer to stampede. The one behind which he was standing might kick out.

Far quicker than it takes to tell, Peaksi saw a picture of what could happen: reindeer in sudden panic; animals rearing, kicking, and himself going off the ice bridge, down into the dark, unplumbed depths of the crevasse.

The sergeant was a brave man, but in that moment he experienced a wave of fear. Before, he had been eager to arrest Johani and Mikkel, keen to return the herd to Gustav Nillson. But now, as he released the pressure on the trigger of his revolver, he was suddenly very frightened. He took half a pace backward and looked over the edge of the ice bridge. Once he looked down, there was only one thing he desired—to get back onto the solid ice of the glacier itself. He turned and walked slowly, cautiously, back across the ice bridge.

Conscious of the wondering glances of the Lapp herders and his own constable, Sergeant Peaksi tried to mask his retreat by bellowing, "Constable Heikki, load your rifle."

Heikki had been standing behind the Lapps, for he did not like the appearance of the ice bridge, and he looked unhappy as he pushed his way to the forefront. He worked the bolt of his rifle, and now there was a cartridge in the breech. Then mechanically he pushed off the safety catch.

"Pick off the deer on the bridge, one by one," Peaksi ordered. "I'm going to take Sarris and his herdsman in, if it's the last thing I ever do."

7

Outlaws!

There were grunts of protest from the Lapps. To shoot reindeer deliberately was a crime in their eyes.

Constable Heikki lifted the rifle and cuddled the butt to his cheek; but before he could fire the first shot, the animal in his sights began to move. Johani had stepped off the bridge, and the reindeer were only too pleased to trot over the last few yards and onto the solid ice of the glacier edge. The constable lowered his rifle and looked questioningly at his superior.

Sergeant Peaksi knew what he ought to do—stride across that narrow pathway of ice and arrest Johani Sarris, now kneeling at the opposite end of the bridge. Peaksi knew what he *should* do, but for the first time since he had been a sergeant he shirked his duty. The crevasse looked wider than it was, the bridge far too narrow. He gulped, conscious that Constable Heikki and the Lapps were staring at him.

Then came the sound of an axe on ice, a swift, almost

75

mechanical *lop . . . lop . . . lop . . . lop . . . lop*. Johani was
on his knees, making chips of ice fly as he hacked at the
bridge end. The axe edge was keen, Johani was strong,
and it was obvious he planned to break down the bridge.

Sergeant Peaksi closed his eyes for a moment, feeling
like a man reprieved from almost certain death. To save
his own dignity he turned to his constable, saying, "All
right, Constable Heikki, you had better not go across
now; the young lunatic will have the bridge down in a
minute." Then in a louder voice he went on: "Sarris,
drop that axe at once. You are only making things worse
for yourself by defying the law. Don't make me lose my
patience completely."

Johani did not even look up, and there were little smiles of satisfaction on the faces of the Lapps standing behind Sergeant Peaksi. Their sympathies were with Johani and they admired his courage. Not one of them would normally have risked taking a herd across the ice bridge. It pleased them to see the three hundred reindeer that had made it safely over the crevasse and were now moving farther away at a trot. The sergeant would not get the Sarris reindeer that day, at least.

"Sarris," Sergeant Peaksi yelled again, "I am going to give you a last chance. Be sensible. Promise me you will bring the herd back to Niklander's settlement and I will see that . . ." Then he stopped, for the bridge was giving him his answer.

There was a sudden creaking and groaning, and Johani stopped chopping away at the deepening channel where his side of the bridge met the solid glacier. Something was happening in the bridge's center. Two or three of the long icicles suddenly snapped off and fell like bullets down into the depths of the crevasse, shining for a moment in the moonlight, then vanishing into the shadows.

Slowly, very slowly at first, a crack began to spread in the middle of the bridge, starting at the bottom and working upward. The groaning and creaking grew more pronounced. The bridge quivered, then suddenly it bent downward at the middle as if it had been hinged there. There were pistol-like cracks from each end as the connection with the two sides of the crevasse snapped. Then the bridge was gone.

"All right," Peaksi thundered, and now that there was no possibility of his having to risk crossing the ice bridge he felt more himself. "I shall give you twenty-four hours to return. If you do not give yourself up, along with the herd, I shall ask permission to outlaw you. You understand? Outlaw you! You know what that means!"

Across the gap Johani looked at the angry sergeant and shook his head. He was now feeling very much happier. He had lost one reindeer down the crevasse, but most of the herd was quietly moving north. He had won.

"If I declare you an outlaw," Peaksi called across, "no one will be able to help you. No one will sell you food; no one will buy hides from you. I shall have word sent around to every Lapp family in the north, warning them that they will be severely punished if they aid you in any way. You know what that means? Starvation for the herd, even if you manage to live."

"It means death to the Sarris herd if I give my reindeer up to the Swedish butcher," Johani countered.

"Sit down for ten minutes, Sarris," Sergeant Peaksi counseled. "Just think it over quietly. You cannot win. Even if you survive the winter, the spring will come and it will be easier for the police to move about then. We shall know where to find you. You are a fool if you continue to defy me."

"I will bring my herd back if you promise not to let Mr. Nillson butcher them," Johani called back. "He can wait until my father returns from the house of the doctor."

"That's impossible," Nillson snapped. "I have bought the reindeer, and if I am to make any money, I must have them now. My customers are waiting for them across the border."

"The Swedish merchant must have his reindeer now, Sarris!" Sergeant Peaksi shouted.

There was no mistaking Johani's answer. He slipped his curl-toed shoes into the thongs of his skis, turned, and began to head north. Anna had been gone several minutes, and Mikkel, smoking solemnly, blew a great cloud of smoke into the air, then, knocking out the ash from his pipe, followed the new master of the Sarris family.

"All right," Sergeant Peaksi said grimly, "we'll just have to bring them in another way. Come on, they've asked for it and they'll get it. No one can escape the law."

Sergeant Peaksi knew that the story of how Johani Sarris had defied the Outlander police would spread throughout the north. Whenever Lapp trails crossed, the story would be told with relish.

"They'll soon see that I can't be beaten," Peaksi told himself as he skied down the snowy slopes toward Niklander's settlement. "Sarris thinks he can lose himself and his herd. I'll show him he can't."

Back at the settlement he had a meal and a few hours' sleep. Then, borrowing a *pulka* and a strong reindeer ox, he started south, taking the same route Johani had used when he went to telephone for the helicopter and the doctor. Johani had been urged along by love of his father, while the policeman was driven by his anger at being defeated. Even so, he did not travel as quickly as the young Lapp.

Once at the Juolfi house he wound the telephone handle until the distant operator answered him. Then he was put through to the sheriff in charge of the district. Very quickly he explained the situation.

"If I could have the use of the ambulance helicopter, sir, I'd soon have the herd back, and young Sarris and his herdsman under lock and key. It would prove to the Lapps that they just will not be allowed to break the law."

"I'm worried about Sarris selling his entire herd," the sheriff grumbled. "They don't normally do that kind of thing, you know, Sergeant."

"But Gustav Nillson has the signed contract, witnessed by Paavo Niklander," Peaksi pointed out. "It is there in black and white. Of course if . . ."

"Call me again in an hour," the sheriff said curtly. "I'll see if I can get through to the hospital. I'd like to hear Sarris' side of the story before I do anything. I know the man and he isn't a fool . . . and he isn't a liar, either."

Sergeant Peaksi hung up, fuming. An hour later he called the sheriff again. This time he got more satisfaction.

"I got through to the hospital," the sheriff said, "but Jouni Sarris is very ill and unable to answer questions. His wife, of course, has no idea what went on when he was selling to Nillson."

"So I can have the helicopter," Sergeant Peaksi said eagerly. "After all," he added, "we can't let the Lapps get away with a thing like this, can we? It is sheer defiance of the law."

"Hm. Yes." The sheriff was far from happy about the matter, but he could see Sergeant Peaksi's point of view. The north was a vast place, and the Lapps had to be made to realize the necessity for laws. After a long mo-

80

ment of hesitation, he said, "I'll call you back tomorrow and let you know about the helicopter. In the meantime I'll try again to see if Sarris can say anything."

"Thank you, sir. I'll get hold of a few forest Lapps to take with me to act as herdsmen," Sergeant Peaksi said. "I can handle Sarris and his man Mikkel, but I will have to have help with the herd. The hill Lapps couldn't be trusted to cooperate; but the forest Lapps will do as they are told."

That afternoon Peaksi contacted four forest Lapps and told them to stand by for a police job. And early the next morning the sheriff called to tell Peaksi that the helicopter was coming—but he could have it for one day only.

Fortunately for Peaksi, the weather was clear. After lighting three fires in a clearing the sergeant rubbed his gloved hands with glee when he heard the first drone of the helicopter's engine, with the accompanying whirr and clatter of its big revolving vanes. Looking up, he saw the stars still shining like chips of illuminated ice in the clear sky.

As gently as if it had been lowered from the sky on the end of a steel hawser, the helicopter came down in the space between the three fires. Sergeant Peaksi climbed aboard and had a talk with the pilot, explaining exactly what was to be done, and where they would probably find the Sarris herd. Together they studied a map, and when the pilot was satisfied, Peaksi called to the forest Lapps.

Four frightened little men came across the clearing and handed up their dogs, their skis, and some packages of stores. Then reluctantly they climbed aboard. Mr.

Juolfi from the post office and rest house building waved to them with his pipe. The engine roar increased, the idling vanes spun more rapidly, and very slowly the helicopter lifted off the snow.

It hung like some huge dragonfly for a few moments at a height of about sixty feet, then began to move north. However ungainly it might appear, there was no doubt about its superiority over even the fastest *pulka*. A good reindeer can make a dozen miles an hour. The helicopter was traveling at more than a mile a minute, which meant that Niklander's settlement was barely half an hour's flying time away.

Sergeant Peaksi would have liked to call at the settlement to pick up his constable, but the pilot shook his head. With six men, four dogs, and packages of food, the helicopter had all the weight it could carry. They passed over the settlement as the first light of the new day was showing in the sky to the southeast.

As the growing light began to spread across the sky, Johani rose from a crouching position, called to his dog, and began to move along the hillside. His skis made a faint hiss and crunch on the frozen surface of the snow. He had been herding for more than twelve hours, and soon it would be time for him to return to the tent in the valley; then Mikkel would take over.

The herd was scattered throughout a wood of dwarf birch. After their near arrest on the glacier, Johani, Anna, and Mikkel had followed the reindeer north to the place where some of the Sarris equipment had been left before the family started south for the round-up. Now this equipment was all down there in the valley: the black shape of the tent, beside it two *pulkas*, and a drying rack on which lay reindeer meat—they had been forced to kill a young bull to augment their food supply. Johani could just make out the little wooden sawhorse and next to it a pile of birch twigs which Anna had collected.

The herd was hardly visible among the birch trees. All the animals were hard at work, digging down through the snow to the moss beneath. Unlike the forest reindeer, which are dainty feeders, the hill reindeer tear out the moss by the roots. Up in the mountains the moss is not so rich, nor so thick in growth. Because of this the herds do not stay in one place very long.

Johani looked up as the croak of a raven sounded in the clear sky. The big carrion-eater flapped slowly across the valley, and a sad look passed over Johani's face. Somewhere, he guessed, a weak animal was in distress; ravens had an uncanny eye for such unfortunates.

The bird flew on out of sight and the silence returned, only to be broken by a new sound which made Johani halt, spraying fine snow from his skis as he did so. The sound was like the purring of a cat, and Johani frowned. Very occasionally an airplane flew over this wild region. Several times Johani had seen white streaks moving high above the top of the highest hills, and the faint murmur of engines had come down to him. If the sun happened to be shining, he could actually see the airplane and he always wondered why men wanted to climb into the air.

But the purring from the south was different. It gradually grew louder, and Johani's thoughts turned to the thing which had passed over him when he had made his mercy dash to the home of Juolfi.

As he stared into the gradually lightening sky he

thought he saw something. It looked like a red dot passing over the end of the valley, miles away. Uneasy, yet not connecting the sound of engines with the police, he went down the hillside, passing quietly through the herd. One or two reindeer looked up, then returned to their task of digging. Even through the deep snow they could smell the lichen which was their main source of food.

The purring died away as the machine passed into the next valley, and Johani's uneasiness faded. He paused to free a cow which had got her antlers locked in the branches of a dwarf birch, then continued across the snow toward the tent. A thin plume of pale blue smoke was curling up from its open top, staining the crystal-clear air.

He was about sixty yards from the tent when, almost as if a door had been opened, the purring began again. This time it came from the north and was much louder.

Johani turned and his dog growled, the hair on its neck and back sticking up, its eyes shining green as they always did when an enemy was about. For a moment Johani was bewildered. The red dot had been at the bottom of the valley; now it had come over the hills and was at the top. He did not realize that Sergeant Peaksi had directed the pilot to take them up a valley parallel to the one where the Sarris herd was feeding. Then the helicopter had hopped over the hilltop. It was like a policeman going up a back street, then through a house and into the front street to cut off the retreat of wrong-doers.

Anna came crawling out of the tent to stare at the helicopter, whose engine now sounded like thunder. The machine seemed to be hanging in the air; but even as they watched, the red blob began to descend at a spot farther up the valley.

"Anna," Johani asked, "is that the—?"

"Yes—yes." Anna did not need to hear the full question. "It is the thing which came for Father. It's brought him back. Oh, Johani—Johani, now everything will be all right."

Mikkel came out of the tent and, catching Anna's last words, looked at her in surprise before shaking his head.

"No, that cannot be true," he muttered. "The doctor said it would be many weeks before your father could come back. He was badly burned, and—"

"But that is the machine which brought the doctor," Anna insisted. "Why should it come again if . . ." Then she paused, a sudden suspicion blanketing the joy in her eyes.

"Suppose it were the Outlander?" Mikkel muttered. "If it is, we are finished."

Johani did not speak. He watched the red-painted helicopter touch down, and squinted his eyes against the snow glare when the door opened and first one, then another man got down onto the snow. Five men in all came out, followed by four dogs. Then bundles of skis and ski sticks and some parcels were heaved out into the snow.

"It is the Outlander policeman," Johani whispered. "And he has brought some herdsmen with him. That is why they have dogs. Mikkel . . ."

Mikkel shrugged. "We might dodge the flying machine, Johani, but we cannot get the herd on the move and away before the Outlander and his men catch up."

Anna hurried into the tent and hastily put some food

85

into a pack, wrapped the iron pot with the reindeer meat she had been cooking for Johani, and came out, her arms full.

Joining Johani and Mikkel, she stood staring up the valley. The four herdsmen were now moving in line toward the top of the birch wood, their dogs at their heels. The parcels which had been handed out of the helicopter must have been packs, for each man now carried one on his back. The fifth man, the police sergeant, was heading down the valley toward the Sarris tent.

"He is coming for us," Mikkel said soberly, "and I suppose we shall go south in the red flying machine, and that will be the end of it all. He is too clever, and has—"

"The end, did you say?" Johani came to sudden life at the words. "Are we to do as he says, like old reindeer cows? He is one and we are three."

"Johani, the Outlander has a gun," Mikkel pointed out. "That is why he is not afraid."

"But will he take us south?" Anna asked anxiously. "I am afraid. They will put us in the stone house, and we shall not be able to walk about. Johani, say something! What can we do? I am frightened."

"What can we do?" Johani asked, and swinging around, he pointed up the hill. "We can go up there. Let the Outlander come up on top after us, and then we shall see who is best."

Mikkel took the pack of food from Anna, and Johani grabbed hold of the soot-blackened cooking pot, still warm from the fire. They were turning away toward the hill when Sergeant Peaksi raised an arm.

"He makes a sign to us," Anna said, but she was wrong.

86

The raised arm was a signal to the pilot of the helicopter that he was no longer needed and could move off. The idling engine suddenly roared to vigorous life and the lazily moving arms swung into a chattering speed. As the thrum of the engine grew deeper, the red-bodied helicopter lifted from the snow.

If the pilot had turned west when he was high enough and gone over the hill into the next valley, all would have been well. Instead, he came swinging down the valley at little more than sixty or seventy feet above the snow. The thunder of his engine echoed and re-echoed from hilltop to hilltop until the noise was such that even Johani, Anna, and Mikkel paused to look back.

They were in time to see reindeer scattering out of the birch wood, terrified by the unaccustomed clamor. The four herdsmen and their dogs were powerless to prevent the stampede. The reindeer ran in all directions: north up the valley, west up the hillside, east into the valley bottom, and south down toward the spot where the Sarris tent stood, a black splash on the white snow.

In five minutes the thunderous clamor had died away. The helicopter was a rapidly disappearing red dot to the south, and the four forest Lapps, with their dogs, were beginning the wearisome task of rounding up the scattered herd.

Then, as the last faint murmur of the helicopter's engine died away, there came a shout from below. Sergeant Peaksi had kept on skiing down the valley, and was now standing by the Sarris tent. He cupped his gloved hands about his mouth and called up to the three fugitives: "You may as well come down now, Sarris. You can't live up there. I've got your sleeping bags, your food, your tent—everything. I'm going to take them all down to Niklander's settlement. Come down and don't be a fool."

Mikkel looked at Johani, and there was despair in the old man's eyes as he said, "He is right, Johani. We have nothing left."

Johani gave Mikkel a steely look, then slowly shook his head. "We have one thing left, Mikkel, and if we go down there we shall lose even that."

"And what have we left?" Anna asked.

"Our freedom," Johani told her, surprise in his voice. "While we have that, and while the herd remains alive, there is hope."

"And can a man live on hope?" Mikkel asked. "Will it keep us warm during the winter? He has our sleeping bags, even the spare sennan grass for our *skaller*."

"But he has not got us," Johani said firmly. "If you wish to go down, Mikkel, go down. I am Johani Sarris, and those are the Sarris reindeer in the valley. My father left them for me to herd."

He moved up the hill a further fifty feet, then sat down. Mikkel and Anna joined him. The tent was plain to see, thin smoke beginning to come from its top again as Sergeant Peaksi built up the fire.

There was silence among the three huddled Lapps until suddenly Johani stiffened and his face lit up.

"Listen," he said eagerly. "It is going to take several hours before the herd is gathered together again. By then it will be dark. The policeman will probably decide to stay for the night in the tent—so!"

"So what?" Anna asked petulantly. "What can we do?"

"We can wait until the glow fades from the top of the

tent and tells us that the policeman is asleep. Then we can go down. He is a man, even if he does wear a silver badge in his fur cap. He will sleep when he is tired, and what use is a gun if a man sleeps?" He looked anxiously at Mikkel. "Do you agree?"

The old herdsman frowned and stared down at his boots as if he were weighing their chances against an armed policeman. Then he began to nod, and looking at Johani, he grinned.

The young Lapp grinned back; Mikkel's support made him feel much more confident. "Anna, pass me the pot, for I am hungry," he said. "You can sleep. Mikkel, you too can rest. I shall keep watch. In a little while the darkness will be here again, and night is our friend."

8

Peaksi's Trick

The meat in the pot was already cold, and there was a
skim of fat on top of what should have been hot soup.
Johani did not worry. He was hungry, and he ate raven-
ously, sticking the point of his knife in and spearing the
reindeer meat. Mikkel ate too. When they had eaten
their fill, Anna finished what was left. It is the custom
that men must have their hunger satisfied first, for they
are the ones who go out into the bitter cold of the winter
to watch the herd.

Very quickly the half-light, which is all the daylight
the Lapps have during the winter months, faded. Stars
grew bright again in the blue-black sky, and the cold
tightened its grip once more. Anna huddled against her
brother, laid her head against his shoulders, and went to
sleep. Mikkel lit his pipe, guarding the flame of his match
with gloved hands so that no light could be seen to give
away their position.

Only Johani remained alert and watchful. His gaze was riveted on the spot below where the tent was pitched. Gradually it became blurred, even against the white of the snowy landscape, and finally the only way he could place it was by the pink glow showing through the opening at the top. Each time fresh birch logs were put on the fire there would be a flurry of sparks shooting upward. When the fire burned low, the red glow became a weak pink.

The hours dragged by, but Johani sat with the patience which seems part of the make-up of every Lapp. There had been no sparks for some time, yet the fireglow showed strongly. At length, however, it started to fade, and he decided that the sergeant must have stoked up the fire, then gone to sleep. Waking Anna and Mikkel, Johani said, "Make sure the dogs can't bark, Mikkel. We'll go down, and I'll peek into the tent. If the policeman has two of the herdsmen in the tent with him, we'll go out into the valley and speak to the men looking after our reindeer. If he's alone, I have another plan, but I think at least two of his herdsmen will be resting with him."

"You say you will talk to the Outlander's herdsmen?" Mikkel scoffed. "What use is talking? They are paid by the Outlander and will do as he says."

"Sometimes talking is better than a blow," Johani pointed out. "After all, we are Lapps and they are Lapps. They might be willing to let us take the herd. It is worth trying."

Mikkel fastened the jaws of the four dogs with thongs, so that they could not bark. Then they went down the hill, carrying their skis. The pale pink light from the top of the tent was their only guide until they were within twenty yards of it, when it was visible as a dark mass against the gray of the snow.

Johani and Mikkel went forward, leaving Anna to hold the dogs. Bending down by the door of the tent, Johani listened carefully. There was no sound whatsoever.

Johani drew his long knife, quietly slit the thongs holding the tent door shut, drew one flap aside, and shoved his head into the tent.

"What is it?" Mikkel asked, hearing Johani's gasp. "Is he dead?"

"He's not here," Johani snapped, and throwing caution to the winds, opened the tent flap all the way. He crept in, with Mikkel at his heels. In silence they stood and stared. Mikkel moved forward and laid his hand on the pile of ashes where the fire had been. They were quite cold, proving that the fire had been out for some hours.

Standing at one side, its glass top covered with what looked like a piece of pink rag, was a flashlight. It was that, shining upward through the top of the tent, which had given the illusion, for several hours, that there was a fire in the tent. Only when the battery began to lose its strength, suggesting to the watching Johani that the fire was dying, had the pink glow begun to fade.

Anna came creeping in shortly afterward. For a few moments she could not understand how Johani had been tricked.

"By the coldness of the ashes," Johani said, kneeling and laying his hand among the gray, powdery flakes, "they must have six or seven hours' start. That is a real Outlander's trick."

"Do you mean that we have lost the herd?" Anna asked, a trace of fear in her voice.

"If they get to Niklander's settlement, yes," Johani said bitterly. "I know that trader will not wait for anything when the reindeer are in the corral. He will start butchering at once."

"But they will not be there yet," Mikkel pointed out. "The herd travels slowly at night, and the moon is only just rising. You and I might stop them if we really wanted to."

"If we *what?*" Johani asked. "You are an old man, Mikkel, or I would call you a fool."

"What I meant was that if we cared to go straight across the hills, we could get to the top of the Narrow Valley before them," Mikkel explained. "And only one animal at a time can come up the Narrow Valley."

Johani pondered for a moment. To make a beeline for the top of the Narrow Valley would entail tremendous physical strain, and there would be much danger. Yet it was the only way.

"All right, Mikkel. We will do that. Anna, you stay here, and—"

"If you go, I go," Anna said firmly. "Two are better than one, and three are better than two. Come, let us not waste time."

Johani stood staring up into the sky. Within a few minutes there should be some moonlight. Later, unless the sky clouded over, the night would be quite light, for the snow always acted as a reflector to the moon. Slipping their feet into the ski thongs, they started down into the valley bottom. In summer it was an impassable bog. Now it was solid, and as smooth as a frozen lake.

Johani led, with Anna behind, Mikkel bringing up the rear, and the dogs on each side. After about half an hour, as they were descending a long slope, Johani began to *joik*. *Joiking* is Lapp singing, with the singer making up the words as he goes along. Often enough the songs are sad, sometimes gay, sometimes wild and fierce. Johani's *joik* sounded like a battle cry, and it lifted the sadness from Anna's heart. She joined in the choruses:

> Policeman drives us off with gun;
> Nun-nun-nuu . . . nun-nun-nuu!
> Forest Lapps help in his fun;
> Nun-nun-nuu . . . nun-nun-nuu!
>
> Sarris reindeer all must go;
> Nun-nun-nuu . . . nun-nun-nuu!
> Vanish like first fall of snow;
> Nun-nun-nuu . . . nun-nun-nuu!
>
> Now comes Sarris, Johan-ee;
> Nun-nun-nuu . . . nun-nun-nuu!
> Mikkel, Anna, making three;
> Nun-nun-nuu . . . nun-nun-nuu!
>
> Driving fast along the track;
> Nun-nun-nuu . . . nun-nun-nuu!
> They will get the reindeer back;
> Nun-nun-nuu . . . nun-nun-nuu!
>
> Then police and forest Lapp;
> Nun-nun-nuu . . . nun-nun-nuu!
> Cry like baby after slap;
> Nun-nun-nuu . . . nun-nun-nuu!

The last verse pleased Anna and Mikkel so much that they kept *joiking* it over and over again, until the start of another hard climb took all the breath they had.

The moon had come out, and climbing high in the sky, it paled the stars with its brilliance. As the three human figures with their dogs crossed a snow-covered glacier, they and their shadows looked like wavering phantoms. They neither talked nor sang; the only sounds came from the faint keening of the skis and the panting of the hard-pressed dogs. Behind them they left a fine powdering of snow, which slowly settled and seemed like vapor in the brilliant light of the moon.

The moon made their cross-country journey possible, revealing the dangers along the way. They recognized crevasses by the faint shadows its light cast, telling of snow lying a little lower than the rest. It was Johani who always took the risk, skirting if the crevasse looked much too wide, taking a flying leap at full speed if he thought it could be crossed.

Uphill they toiled like madmen, panting, perspiring, but never halting. On the downhill swoops Johani's voice lifted in triumphant *joiks*, reassuring him that they must succeed and helping to keep up Anna's courage when her muscles began to tire.

Though Johani had no compass, he succeeded in bringing Anna and Mikkel out on the very edge of the glacier which they had crossed three days earlier—the glacier cut by the big crevasse. Down in the valley to the left they could see the tiny pink spot of a fire. It was like a signal of hope, for it told them that the herd could not yet have come up the Narrow Valley.

"Coffee for the policeman," Johani chuckled. "He is so sure we are beaten."

"No Lapp would stay down there now," Mikkel agreed, "for I can smell snow. It is getting warmer."

"All the better for us," Johani said. "You know what to do. If they start the herd up the Narrow Valley you must stop—"

"I can see something now," Anna whispered. "Look."

She was right. Like ghosts, the first reindeer were coming along the bottom of the knife-slash of a pass known as the Narrow Valley. At once Mikkel turned to the right, Johani and Anna to the left. It would be Mikkel's task to hold the pass, while the others dealt with Sergeant Peaksi. How, they did not yet know.

9

The Wolf Howls

Mikkel crossed the big crevasse with one hand touching a silver coin hung about his throat by a piece of string. It was a lucky coin given to him long, long ago by his mother.

The very narrow snow bridge he used shook so much that when he reached the middle he halted, his heart beating rapidly. His fingers tightened around the smooth silver coin, and it seemed to give him courage. Quietly, one foot at a time, he crossed the rest of the bridge. It started to fall even as he got his left foot on firm ice again. For a moment he hung there, knowing that the slightest wrong move would cost him his balance and his life.

Leaning forward, he carefully swung his right leg across the last bit of gaping space until his foot found the safety of the solid glacier. Then he paused and looked back. The moon was lighting the crevasse for some thirty feet, but below that was inky darkness. The old man gripped the silver coin even tighter, and whispered a little prayer of thankfulness. He gulped, slid forward a few yards, then pulled on his glove.

He sped as fast as any startled reindeer across the top of the glacier, and down the steep slope by the side of the snout. A few minutes later he was standing at the top of the Narrow Valley itself. Down there something was moving; but he knew from past experience that moonlight was tricky. A frightened man could see enemies; a man given the task of turning back a herd might see tossing antlers where none existed.

Mikkel went cautiously down the narrow trail, keeping his body bent so that the shadow he threw was only a small one. Half way down he stopped and listened. Faintly but clear on the bitterly cold air came the *clackclackety-clack* of reindeer hoofs and the dull *tong-kolong-kong* of a herd bull's bell.

The bell was faint, sign that the herd was moving slowly. It was tired after being driven hard, and the Narrow Valley was a steep trail.

Mikkel squatted, with his ski stick between his legs acting as a stool to take his weight. He filled his lungs, threw back his head, and a moment later the air was trilling to the long-drawn-out howl of a wolf. Only those who have heard a wolf or a husky dog baying the moon can understand the blood-chilling threat such a howl carries. It can make the bravest man halt in his tracks. It will send a defenseless animal seeking immediate shelter.

After that shattering *Aaaaaoooooowowowowowowowoooooo* the hills took up the cry, and it was whispered from icy peak to icy peak, growing softer each time until it died away in the far distance.

Mikkel listened. When his first call had died away, there was only silence, a silence so deep that the sound of snow crunching a little under his left ski seemed almost thunderous.

There was no *clack-clackety-clack-clack* now, no steady *tong-kolong-kolong-kong*. The advancing herd had stopped.

Mikkel moved farther down and called again. In the moonlight, brilliant though it was, he could see nothing. The herd had merged with the snow and were as invisible to him as if they were ghosts. Now, however, his keen ears were picking up faint sounds: the grunt of a herd bull, the muffled low of a cow separated from her calf in the confusion reigning on that narrow trail. The leaders were trying to turn back. Yet those far down were still trying to move up, urged on by the Lapp herders. It was a complete block.

From down the Narrow Valley came a bellowed *Aw-aw-aw-awawawwwwwwww!*—the call of a Lapp herdsman to his reindeer to get moving. Mikkel answered it with another wolf howl. This time it was the sharp, excited call of a hunting wolf. There were some in the herd who had heard calls like that before, and smelled the blood of their companions.

The leading reindeer made a frenzied attempt to retreat down the Narrow Valley, and the calls of the herdsman behind them had no effect at all. Mikkel heard the man and his dog. Breaking through the icy crust on the snow, the old man scooped up handful after handful of the powdery white stuff below the frozen surface and threw it on himself.

It was so fine that some of it floated away like powder. The rest stuck on Mikkel's blue *kofte*, changing him in a minute from a dark blur on the moonlit snow to something which could have been a shadow, or even a phantom.

He moved down toward the herd, and now he could see the tossing antlers of the cows and oxen near the front. The antler points caught the moonlight, reflecting it dully, so that there seemed to be a forest of them moving this way and that.

The oncoming herdsman was shouting, trying to get the nervous beasts moving again, and also hoping that his voice would send the unseen wolf on its way.

A command sent the herdsman's dog scampering and slipping out on the steep hillside, so that if the wolf were skulking there, its presence would soon be made known.

Aw-aw-aw-aw-aw . . . The Lapp was calling again as he swung to the head of the herd. *Aw-aw-aw-a* . . . The calling stopped abruptly. Seen for a second in the moonlight as a vague snakelike thing, Mikkel's lasso leaped in flickering coils, the loop settling over the herdsman's head and shoulders. The old man pulled the lasso tight in a second. The dog, sensing something wrong, raced across and flung itself at Mikkel as he bent over his prisoner.

Only a man who had handled herd dogs for a lifetime could have done what old Mikkel did then. Just as the open jaws seemed about to close on his wrist, the whole arm moved, and a second later the dog was rolling over and over in the snow. Mikkel snapped a command to it and the dog slunk away, its drooping tail and pressed-down ears seeming to offer an apology for having tried such foolishness.

"We'll go down and see what your master is doing," Mikkel said when he had made sure the herdsman could not get free. "If you make a sound, I shall have to take off your *skaller* and leave you sitting in the snow."

A grunt from Mikkel's prisoner signified that the man understood and agreed to keep silent. Had the reindeer-hide *skaller* been taken off, frostbite would quickly have done its work on his bare feet.

In the valley bottom Sergeant Peaksi sat on the Sarris *pulka* while one of his herdsmen prepared a fire. The first of the reindeer were already starting up the Narrow Valley and, since they had to travel in single file, Sergeant Peaksi decided there was ample time for a fire to be lit and coffee made. He was hungry, thirsty, and tired.

He watched while the forest Lapp kindled the fire from some of the wood brought along from the Sarris encampment. The Sarris coffee kettle was put over the flames hung on a forked stick, and some of the sergeant's own coffee was slipped into the pot. He liked his coffee to come gently to the boil, to get the last ounce of flavor from it.

From a tube which looked as if it might contain toothpaste, the sergeant squeezed a generous helping of condensed, sweetened milk, while the Lapp stared in amazement.

"None of your curded milk from the belly of a long-dead reindeer, my friend," Peaksi chuckled. "One day you Lapps might learn how much better it is to live like civilized people."

He lifted the bubbling kettle of coffee from the fire and filled first his enamel mug, then the wooden cup of

101

the Lapp herder. He drew back as the hot enamel burned his lips; but the Lapp drank almost immediately, since the wooden cup did not heat up so quickly.

"You must have a mouth of brass," Peaksi said, blowing on his coffee. "I don't know how . . ." Then he stopped, for from up the Narrow Valley had come the long-drawn-out call of a wolf.

The Lapp herdsman drained his wooden cup, looked longingly at the kettle for a moment, then rose to his feet. He put on his skis.

"Better that I go and help," he said. "Sometimes there are half a dozen wolves, and if the herd is attacked . . ." He shrugged.

"Yes, off you go, I don't want more trouble," Peaksi said, still blowing on his coffee. He watched the Lapp move off, then muttered: "I don't know why I should have to spend my life among a people who live eight months in freezing cold, and then for four months are bitten to death by millions of mosquitoes. This is a land God forgot, I think. If He . . ." A faint sound in the air made him half turn, spilling some of his precious coffee. The Lapp herdsman was already speeding away, and he did not see the sergeant suddenly fall over backward as a skillfully thrown lasso tightened about him, pinning his arms to his sides.

Anna, who had been standing ready, rushed in and clapped her soft fur cap over the sergeant's face, choking off what would have been an angry shout. Johani had handled many an angry bull reindeer at the end of a lasso, and he had no difficulty with the police sergeant.

Turned face down in the snow, too bewildered to put up an effective struggle, Peaksi had his wrists drawn behind his back and secured by thongs of reindeer hide. Jerked to a sitting position, he was effectively gagged by his own fur collar. Johani pulled it up and fastened it to overlap across his mouth, and for the second time since taking the oath as a policeman, Sergeant Peaksi was powerless to move or speak.

"Take his cap, Anna," Johani ordered, "and be sure to wear it so that the silver badge is at the front where it will show in the moonlight."

Johani took Sergeant Peaksi's revolver, and in doing so disturbed the fur collar, temporarily removing the gag.

"Sarris," Sergeant Peaksi stormed. "You must be crazy to do a thing like this. Untie my hands at once. If I report this to headquarters, they'll send you to prison for the rest of your life. For life, you understand? I'll make you wish you'd never been born. I'll—"

"The puppy yaps until the wolf turns on him," Johani said quietly. "Be quiet or I shall not put Anna's cap over your head and ears. Would you like to know how frost-bitten ears feel?"

Sergeant Peaksi relaxed. In any of the small settlements where traders set up their stores and the Lapps came in to buy supplies, his silver badge was as good as any weapon. Men respected him, listened to him, did as he told them. He was the law! Now these two youngsters, a boy of sixteen and his fifteen-year-old sister, were proving that in this land, where only reindeer, wild animals, and Lapps could live, the silver badge in his astrakhan hat was not enough.

He sat stiffly erect as Anna placed her own cap over his head and about his ears. Nor did he protest when

Johani folded the gag about his mouth again. He was eased onto the laden *pulka,* and then was dragged a few yards to the rear. Johani took two of their own fur *peskes* which had been taken from their tent, along with other equipment, and covered the irate sergeant.

"That will keep you warm, Mr. Policeman," he chuckled. Then he turned to Anna. "You must sit by the fire and keep your head down a little so that your face will not be recognized. But the cap badge will shine in the moonlight. Here, take the sergeant's gun. You can hold it so that it will be seen. If any of the herders come, they will be more convinced by the gun than anything else that you are the Outlander."

Anna very gingerly took the gun. "Johani, what must I do with it? If somebody comes, I could not shoot them."

"Don't even hold the little thing which makes it work," Johani ordered. "Just sit and let them see the gun."

Going back to the *pulka,* he said, "Now, Mr. Policeman, I want you to shout for the man who has just gone away. Call him back." Johani then gently eased the gag from Sergeant Peaksi's mouth.

"I shall call no one," Peaksi spluttered indignantly. "And I warn . . ." He stopped then, for Johani had whipped off the fur cap.

"You used everything the clever Outlander people have," Johani pointed out, "and with the red thing which flies you stole our herd. So I must use the things we Lapps use."

"You know I shall get frostbitten ears if you do not give me a cap," Peaksi protested.

"You will not get frostbite if you call the herdsman." Johani was inflexible.

Peaksi sat for a moment or so, his lips a thin line, his eyes as frosty as the moon.

"Very well," he said, already feeling his ears cold. "I will call him; but I warn you. Everything you do to me you will pay for. I am a police sergeant, and you—"

"Are you going to call the herdsman?" Johani asked, keeping Anna's cap poised above the sergeant's head.

Peaksi called until there was an answer from where the reindeer were milling around near the foot of the Narrow Valley. Up the valley Mikkel had given his wolf call again and again, and there was chaos on the narrow track as the frightened reindeer tried to turn back but were prevented from retreating by those farther down, which were being urged on by the Lapp herdsmen.

A man came skiing swiftly from among the animals and sped across to where Anna sat by the fire, her head bent a little, the firelight playing on the gun she held.

When she lifted her head as the herdsman came to a halt before the fire, the man stood petrified. He did not know Anna, for he was a forest Lapp, while she lived in the hills.

"Stand still," Johani ordered, and coming forward he went behind the goggle-eyed Lapp and trussed his wrists together, using the man's own lasso. Seating him by the side of Anna he told him to call another of the men.

It was so simple, yet so very effective, Anna sitting there with the gun, her head bent so that the moonlight glistened on the silver badge in the impressive-looking astrakhan fur cap. The second man was trussed like the first with no fuss at all.

Again the captured Lapp was ordered to call yet another of the herdsmen and, after a pause of a few min-

utes, the man started across from the herd. He was full
of apologies and explanations as he came racing up. "I
have shouted up there for Per Gaut, and he does not
reply. I am . . ."

He stopped and swung away, for Anna had lifted her
head a little too soon and the Lapp could see she was not
Sergeant Peaksi. Johani was crouched behind the two
prisoners and as the man turned away, the lasso, which
had already proved its worth with Sergeant Peaksi, hissed
out again.

The Lapp must have sensed its coming, for he thrust
up an arm to fend it off, but the loop dropped neatly

over it and about his neck. A shout he was just starting was choked off as the loop tightened.

Johani was apologetic when he helped the man to his feet and back to the fire. He and his fellows sat side by side in the ruddy glow, their dark faces showing their bewilderment and not a little fear. Lapps are a friendly people; quarrels and fighting are almost unknown among them. The four herdsmen had not been told what they were wanted for when Sergeant Peaksi engaged them to bring a herd down from the hills. Now they were wondering what it was all about.

Johani ordered the first prisoner to call the fourth man, and the cry "Per Gaut—Per Gaut" rang through the air time after time, but without being answered. The reindeer at the foot of the pass were now beginning to spread out, and as those already in the Narrow Valley found there was room to turn back, they did so.

The forest Lapps' dogs had come around to the fire, and there was a minute or so of fighting before they and the Sarris dogs were persuaded to keep the peace.

Suddenly, without any warning sound, Mikkel walked into the firelight. The old man was chuckling delightedly, and there was a twinkle in his eyes as he noted the obvious bewilderment on the faces of Johani and Anna. Had he been an armed enemy he could have turned the tables on them with ease. "I have one man with his hands tied," Mikkel said, "and you have three men—where is the policeman?"

"Resting on the *pulka*," Johani chuckled. "It is important to keep him warm."

Mikkel went off and was back within a few minutes with his prisoner, plus the man's dog, a green-eyed beast which looked as if it had more than three parts wolf in its make-up. It was, however, obviously afraid of Mikkel.

"One day when I am tired of herding reindeer," Mikkel said, bending over and sniffing appreciatively at the coffeepot, "I shall go south. Once at Bossekop there was a man who told us that people earn their meat and a bed by imitating birds. I ought to be well fed for my wolf howls, eh?"

The four forest Lapps looked sharply at Mikkel, then one grinned sheepishly and shook his head. The others also began to grin as they realized how they had been deceived. Then the last man, Per Gaut, asked what all the business was about. Johani told them how it was said the Sarris herd had been sold—three hundred out of a herd of about three hundred and fifty.

Per Gaut shook his head dubiously.

"We did not know about this," he confessed. "But anyway, can a man refuse to do what a policeman asks?"

"We did," Anna said quietly. "We had to, or lose our herd."

"But what can we do now?" Per Gaut asked. "These Outlander policemen are very stern. If we disobey them —well, they take people away to the south, and men stay a long time in a big house. Sometimes they do not come back at all."

"But what is this *house* like?" Anna asked. "I have heard people talk about it. Is it a big house, like the house which was burned down—Paavo Niklander's house?"

"I have never seen it," the spokesman confessed. "But I have heard people talk. It is different from ordinary houses. It is stone, they say, and there are many small rooms no bigger than a Lapp tent. I knew a man who went away with the policeman—he had stolen many reindeer. He was a bad man. They put him away in this big house, a prison is the name, I think. There a man must do only what he is told, and each night he is fastened in a small place. The man I knew was never the same again —always silent and frightened."

Anna's eyes were large with terror as she looked across the fire at her brother.

"Johani, what can—"

"You worry too quickly, Anna," he said, smiling. "We have only to keep out of the way of the policeman until our father and mother return, then all will be well. They will tell the policeman that they did not sell the herd to this Gustav Nillson. Then even the policeman will be glad we did not let the herd be butchered."

Mikkel, who had lived for some time with the Finnish Army during the war against the Russians, and later against the Germans, shook his head doubtfully. He knew something of policemen, breaking the law, and contracts written on paper.

"These Outlanders are great people for what is written down," he pointed out. "After all, Nillson showed us the paper which said he had bought three hundred head, and Paavo Niklander was there to say he was telling the truth. He said he had seen the money paid over."

"Niklander must have been telling a lie," Johani said scornfully. "Surely you must know my father would never sell three hundred of our herd? Only a man who was mad in the head would do such a thing."

Mikkel pursed his lips and again shook his head slowly. "I know, I know," he agreed. "There is a mistake, but these Outlander police—"

Anna stopped them both with an angry "Talk, talk, talk. It dries the throat and settles nothing. Let us eat. I am hungry and I want some coffee."

While Johani built up the fire, Anna went to the *pulka* and rummaged among their pitifully small stores for coffee and reindeer meat. She cooked a meal, and the coffee brought nods of satisfaction from the forest Lapps, for the milk was their own curded milk, dropped in lumps to melt slowly in the strong black brew.

"What about the policeman?" Anna asked. "Perhaps he is hungry."

"He can eat afterward," Johani said, winking at the four forest Lapps. "If we loose him now, he might start shouting at our friends and they would not like that because they are going soon, aren't you?"

The Lapps looked worried, but decided to forget Sergeant Peaksi until they had eaten. It was when the meal was finished and they had all eaten more than two pounds of reindeer meat each, that the question of what the four Lapps should do came up again.

Johani had been thinking hard; he picked up the sergeant's revolver, and there was a smile on his face as he said, "I know you would like to help Sergeant Peaksi, but what can you do when Johani Sarris has the sergeant's gun? You have wives and children, and you want to go back to look after your own reindeer—eh?"

Four heads nodded agreement, but they were jerked around when an angry bellow came from Sergeant Peaksi on the *pulka*. By dint of much struggling and wriggling, the policeman had worked his mouth free of the tightly drawn fur collar, and he made a last desperate effort to get assistance.

"I have heard everything that has been said," he yelled. "I order you four men to set me free. Set me free and keep Sarris and his sister there for me to deal with."

The four forest Lapps were dumbfounded. Living less

nomadic lives than the hill Lapps, they were visited more often by the police, especially during the winter when they lived in small settlements and the police knew where to find them.

Sergeant Peaksi knew he had made an impression, for now he addressed one of the men by name.

"Per Gaut, come and cut me free. You know what will happen to you if you help Johani Sarris and his sister. They have broken the law. It is your duty to help me arrest them and return the stolen herd to its owner."

The forest Lapps looked pathetically anxious, and Per Gaut held out his hands appealingly to Johani as he asked in a whisper, "What can I do? If I refuse to help the policeman, he will punish us. I have a wife and children; my herd will . . ." Then he stopped, his anxiety changing to astonishment, for Johani had whipped out his big knife. Holding it by the handle for a moment, he tossed the knife quickly into the air, caught it by the tip of the blade, then held it out, saying: "There you are; cut the policeman free. When you have done that, you and your friends will be rewarded—but the Sarris family will be dead."

He stopped, then went on very quietly: "What is any Lapp family without its reindeer? What will happen to my father and mother when they come back? There will be no tent; no reindeer to give them meat, milk, hides, clothing. There will be neither son nor daughter to welcome them, for the policeman will have taken us south."

Per Gaut looked at Johani, then dropped his gaze to the knife. Slowly extending his hand, he gripped the handle. Johani released his hold on the blade and with a shrug sat down beside Anna.

111

10

The Herd That Vanished

For perhaps a minute Per Gaut held the knife, the blade glinting in the moonlight.

Anna rose, her eyes flashing scornfully. She stared at Per Gaut, then at each of his three companions, her eyes boring into them so that one after the other they turned their own eyes downward. Mikkel's eyes were watering, but it was impossible to tell whether it was from tears or the cold. Then came a shout from Sergeant Peaksi: "Per Gaut, what are you waiting for? There are four of you. Cut me free."

Per Gaut looked up, sighed, then stepped forward, helped Johani to his feet and returned the knife, saying, "A Lapp's knife is his friend. Why should I use yours to finish you off? May the Sarris family live long and their herd increase until the snow is black with them in winter. *Bazza derivan.*"

As Per Gaut turned to reach for his skis, Johani caught

him by the arm. Lifting a finger to his lips for silence, the young Lapp said in a loud, angry voice, "I shall not come with you, and I shall not let you free the policeman. I have the gun; you can take your skis, your dogs, and go."

In a whisper Johani went on: "It is better for the policeman to think I forced you to go away without helping him. If he thinks that, he will not want to punish you."

Per Gaut lifted a gloved hand to his mouth to choke back a loud guffaw. His three companions were grinning. They could appreciate a joke, and they understood that Johani had now made it impossible for the angry Peaksi to lay any blame on their shoulders.

Per Gaut put a hand on Anna's arm and chuckled softly. "Your brother is a clever one. Too clever for the policeman. This will make a fine tale to tell later on. *Bazza derivan*, Anna Sarris."

"*Mana derivan*," Johani and Anna whispered together, while Mikkel stood on one side, his eyes twinkling.

When the four men were out of earshot Anna turned to her brother, shaking her head to show her bewilderment. "Sometimes, Johani Sarris, I do not understand you. You hand Per Gaut your knife—suppose he had gone to cut the policeman free!"

Johani shook his head. "He would not have done that, Anna. He is a Lapp, as we are Lapps. Would he like it to be told, when Lapp people meet, that he handed Johani and Anna Sarris to the Outlander policeman? I don't think any Lapp would do such a thing. As it is, we have made four friends. They will tell this tale wherever they go. People will laugh, and believe in us. That is what we want—friends and more friends."

He smiled at his sister, winked at Mikkel, then went back to their prisoner. Dragging the *pulka* across to the fire, he cut the sergeant free, ordered Anna to make coffee and Mikkel to round up the herd, which had started to stray in its search for moss.

When Peaksi had rubbed his wrists and ankles, Johani gave him back his revolver. It was not what the sergeant had expected, and he looked up in surprise.

"Changed your mind, eh? Well, you are wiser than you know, Sarris. If you had tried to get the herd away again, it would have meant disaster for it. Everyone is preparing for a very bad winter. There is not enough moss in the hills for the herds. You might have lived, but without transporting fodder from the forest Lapps, your herd would have starved to death."

Johani merely shrugged, while Peaksi went on grimly: "And don't think you could have bought fodder. If I had returned without the reindeer, word would have gone out at once to all Lapp families ordering them not to sell, lend, or give you a thing. Not a spoonful of coffee, not enough feed for one small cow. What made you change your mind?"

"I have not changed my mind," Johani said quietly. "When you have had a meal and I know you are fit to travel south—alone—then Anna and Mikkel and I will take the Sarris herd north. We shall never give them up."

Anna handed the sergeant a cup of coffee, and he drank a little before looking up again at Johani to say, "It is too late to think of that, Sarris. You gave me back my revolver. Now you will do as you are told."

114

Sergeant Peaksi finished his coffee, but there was a thoughtful expression on his face. This Sarris lad was a tougher opponent than he had expected; there might be trouble.

An hour later Anna packed the *pulka* to her liking. The ashes of the fire were already cold. The herd was restive, for there had been two or three flurries of snow, foretaste of a storm blowing up, and Sergeant Peaksi was beginning to worry.

"Tell your herder to start the reindeer toward the Narrow Valley, Sarris," he ordered. "I don't like the looks of the weather."

"We are not going that way," Johani said firmly. "If you mean to shoot me for disobeying your commands, then shoot me now. It is better to shoot a man face to face than to shoot him in the back. That is the way of a weakling."

"Why, you . . ." Sergeant Peaksi spluttered with indignation. Then he pushed the muzzle of his gun into Johani's ribs. "You are playing a dangerous game, Sarris, and I have had enough of it. I am empowered to shoot anyone who resists arrest; that it what you are talking of doing. Now, for the last time, order your herder to lead the reindeer up the Narrow Valley."

When Johani shook his head, the exasperated sergeant turned to Anna. "Listen, girl," he said curtly, "if your brother attempts to move this herd north, I shall shoot him. If you have any sense, you will persuade him that he must come to Niklander's settlement and bring the reindeer with him."

Anna shook her head slowly, deliberately. "In this land the head of the family must be obeyed. While our

115

mother and father are not here, Johani is the head. We do as he says. It is the Lapp way."

She took the single thong of reindeer hide, which is the only rein used when driving a *pulka*, and moved nearer her impatient reindeer ox. He wanted to be off, for the herd was already on the move, heading into the wind as is the way of reindeer.

"I'm giving you a last chance, Sarris," Peaksi said, and to add weight to his threat, he pushed the gun muzzle even more firmly into Johani's ribs. "You are coming back with me if I have to drag your dead body through the snow."

"*Mana derivan,* Anna," Johani said. "Look after the herd."

A fresh flurry of snow hid the moon, and from the darkness came the long-drawn-out call from Mikkel of *Aw-aw-aw-aw-w-w-w-w-w-w-w!*—the call to the herd to start moving.

"All right, Sarris," Peaksi snapped. "I'll take *you* in, anyway. I don't think that sister of yours will get far with the herd. She can't do it with only the old man to help. Go on, get moving."

Johani looked around for a moment. Snow was coming. The thick flakes drifting down were, he sensed, the fore-runners of wind-driven particles, fine and cutting to the face, the kind of snow which blew in great white clouds and drifted. It filled the hollows, wiped out landmarks. If they could have got away now, they might have faded into the wilderness and been lost completely so far as Sergeant Peaksi was concerned.

The herd was now on the move, the individual reindeer looking more like ghosts than ever, with snow clinging to the long hairs under their throats and steam puffing in clouds from their nostrils. Their hoofs provided a soft background music of *clack-clack-clackety-clack,* while from the unseen herd bull in the lead the *kong-long-kolong-ong* of the bell sounded like phantom music.

"Get moving, I said," Sergeant Peaksi repeated, and again jabbed his gun muzzle into Johani's side. "Head for the Narrow Valley—*you* aren't going north!"

They headed west, and in a minute or so could have been completely alone in a world of thickening snow. The first gently falling flakes, big and soft, had been replaced by smaller flakes, coming down now almost like hail. They made a hissing sound on Johani's Four Winds cap and got down his neck, forcing him to close his big stiff collar.

The sound of the bell was lost, even the clacking of hoofs was hardly more than a whisper in the increasing velocity of the wind-driven snow. The moonlight was now only intermittent, shining for seconds, then blanketed by the clouds which were racing across the sky and hurrying, it seemed, to close up the gaps through which the moon could shine.

"Stop," Peaksi ordered. "I think we'll be better fastened together. Get your lasso off; I'm not going to let you give me the slip again."

"No one can slip away in the Narrow Valley," Johani reminded him. "There is one track, and only a bird could get off that, with the snow and ice as they are."

He started to lift the looped lasso from his shoulder and chest, and as he did so there was a sudden rush of silent figures—dogs and a man. They were like ghost creatures, snow-covered and silent.

117

Sergeant Peaksi was half turning when the first dog struck him. The gun in his right hand belched flame, a single yard-long stab of pink which lit up the falling snow for an instant, then went out, making the darkness seem even more black. In that moment of vivid light, however, bared fangs and glowing eyes were visible. It would have struck terror in anyone's heart.

The weight of the dog threw Peaksi off balance, and to a man wearing skis that is fatal: he must fall. Yelling, half in fright and half in anger, the sergeant reeled, lifted one ski awkwardly, fired again, and then flopped over on his side.

He thought he was being attacked by wolves, and crossed his arms over his throat and face. Hunching his body, he rolled over, presenting his back to the enemies. Then he heard a single word of command. If Mikkel had not broken the silence to call off his dogs, Sergeant Peaksi would never have known that the attack was engineered by the old man.

When the sergeant finally got to his feet he managed to find his fur cap, but his gun was lost and one of his ski straps was broken. To the wind's eerie moaning was now added the whispering of minute crystals of snow as they hit the frozen surface, skidded along, and began to fill in the ski tracks.

Sergeant Peaksi had served five winters in Lapland. He was experienced, and he wasted no time now. After hastily repairing the ski strap, he brought out his luminous-dial compass. Ten minutes later he was moving slowly up the Narrow Valley. Once at the top, he could turn his back to the north wind and be at Niklander's settlement in an hour or so.

"And then," he told himself, "things are going to start. I just cannot afford to let them get away with this. I'll ask for four or five more men, and if I don't bring in Sarris and his half-starved herd within a month, I'll resign."

The snowstorm which had helped Mikkel get Johani away from Sergeant Peaksi was the first of a series which whistled down from the Pole for ten days. One withering storm followed another. Hollows were filled in, and the wind blew rocky hilltops bare, leaving them black against a world of white. Sometimes the cold shook the thermometer down to 80° below zero.

In the long valley known as the Loktajaurre the Sarris tent was the only black thing. Beside the tent the top of a half-buried birch tree provided a perch for three Siberian jays and two balls of puffed-out feathers which were tits. The birds had not moved for hours, when suddenly one of the jays shook its feathers and looked toward the black cone which housed the humans. Something was stirring within.

After a minute or so blue smoke began to drift up from the open tent top. Inside, her face lit by the flames of the birch-bark shavings, Anna was wrapped in her best fur *peske* against the bitter cold. Johani and Mikkel were still fast asleep, wrapped from head to foot, their sleeping bags powdered with the snow which had drifted in through the tent top during the hours the fire had been out.

There was only reindeer meat for the pot. No coffee, no sugar, no flour to bake bread against the fire. Even the salt was almost finished.

Johani awoke and went out. He was gone an hour, and came back when the stew was almost ready. His face was grave as he sat down, the warmth of the fire thawing the snow on his reindeer-hide leggings.

"I will go to look for the Aikio family. We must have a load of moss for the herd or they will die. The snow is deep and frozen, and the moss is thin."

Anna nodded. Mikkel shook his head gloomily.

"Remember what the policeman said, Johani," he warned. "Word will have gone around that no one must sell or give to us."

"The Aikios will not let us lose our herd," Johani said confidently. "My father helped them in the past."

When he had finished his meal he brought in one of the reindeer oxen and harnessed it to a *pulka*. Anna had prepared some meat for him, since he did not know exactly where to look for the Aikio family. In a winter which follows a bad summer the herds roam far in search of reindeer moss.

Johani drove the *pulka* along the flat stretches, and led the ox when the passes were steep. The only sounds he heard came from a raven which hung in the air unseen, croaking a warning, following him in the hope that he might have an accident.

Twenty hours after leaving the Sarris tent Johani found the Aikio family. There were four tents, many *pulkas,* and the snow was pitted throughout a huge valley with the lanes and trenches dug by the family's hungry reindeer. Even the big oxen were sometimes almost hidden, so deep had they dug to get down to the moss on which their lives depended.

The dogs rushed out to snarl at Johani, but he drove them off easily, then waited outside the largest tent. The sky was graying for the new day, a day which would last only an hour or so, for it was almost mid-December.

When the tent door opened and Mother Aikio came out, she stared for a moment, then nodded to a small pile of reindeer moss. It was an invitation for Johani to unharness his ox, feed it, then enter the tent.

Once inside the tent, warm from the heat of a glowing fire, Johani sat down opposite fat, jolly-looking Mother Aikio. She had already pushed the coffee kettle into the flames and was grinding beans in her coffee mill.

"Pekka is out with a visitor," she announced, throwing a handful of coffee into the pot and adding a generous helping of salt to it. "You are an important person these days, Johani Sarris."

"Important?" Johani asked, taking off his sodden *skaller* and then spreading the damp sennan grass before the fire. He flexed his bare toes and was glad to feel the heat of the fire on them. "When has the son of Jouni Sarris been important, except to his father, mother, and sister?"

"When Outlander policemen come searching in winter for a man who is barely past his boyhood, then he is important," Mother Aikio murmured. "There is talk of payment, as much as the value of ten reindeer, for anyone who will tell the police where the Sarris family and their herd are."

Johani's heart sank. Ten reindeer! He looked at the brown-faced woman sitting across the fire and wondered. She was not looking at him now but was scooping a generous ball of curded milk from her container. Dropping the milk into the coffee, she chopped off a piece of sugar from a cone. Then, as Johani pulled the coffeepot toward him and took the wooden cup from his belt, she sent a stab of fear through him with the comment, "We knew you were coming, Johani Sarris, for one of the herdsmen saw your fire during the night. When he recognized you, he came here to tell my husband."

Johani sipped the coffee, thinking hard before he asked, "And why did he do this, Mother Aikio? Why did he not come to rest by my fire for a while?"

Mother Aikio shrugged her fat shoulders. "Because there is this matter of ten reindeer. The Outlander police

122

are all over the place—how many new ones there are I cannot say. Three have been here in the past six days."

Johani drank and then refilled his cup. Mother Aikio passed over some cold meat and a piece of her own bread. Johani ate the bread first. He had not had any for nearly two weeks.

He had just taken his second bite when Mother Aikio exploded her bombshell. "There is a policeman out now with my husband, Pekka." Then her face broke into a grin. "Pekka hurried him away to look at the herd because we knew you would be coming. So you can take off your *kofte* and rest."

Johani's shoulders sagged with relief. He had been half afraid that he had walked into a trap, yet wondered at this jolly-faced woman he had known since baby days. She and his mother had been great friends. Not for twenty reindeer, he was sure, would she deliver him to the police.

"I came to see if I could buy reindeer moss," he said between mouthfuls of meat and bread. "Our herd is . . ." He stopped, for Mother Aikio was shaking her head.

"The police are keeping careful watch. Round and round and round they are going, making sure that none of us help you. They are stern. We are not to sell, give, or even lend anything."

"Then we shall surely lose our herd," Johani said glumly. "If we come from our hiding-place, where the moss is thin and being quickly eaten away, the police will find us, and if they . . ." He half turned toward the tent door. Outside the dogs were barking fiercely.

"It is Pekka," Mother Aikio assured him. "He has . . ." She stopped, for her husband was speaking, and there

123

was another voice. Even without seeing the second speaker Johani knew it must be a policeman. He spoke Lapp, but with that accent which left no doubt at all that he was an Outlander.

"Well, we'll go in and see if there is coffee," Pekka was heard saying. Johani looked desperately at Mother Aikio, and she waved a hand to the side of the tent. Lying there, snoring, was one of the older boys of the family. He had been out herding and was now so fast asleep that even if someone walked on him it would bring only a grunt.

Johani slithered across the tent, and the reindeer hides which covered a mat of birch-bark twigs rustled under him. He was just lying down when Pekka thrust open the tent door, pausing there for a moment, his dark, keen eyes peering into the firelit gloom.

His wife waved a hand to indicate Johani, and Pekka turned to spit out into the snow. It gave her a moment or so of grace to rise and cover Johani with a sleeping bag.

When the policeman followed Pekka Aikio into the tent Johani was covered and snoring softly.

"Two sleepers!" the policeman commented, screwing up his eyes against the smoke which now and again filled the tent as a fitful gust of wind blew it back from the open top.

"There is always someone sleeping in a Lapp tent," Mother Aikio said with a laugh. "Only the wife cannot sleep. Always she is cooking, or fetching wood for the fire, or mending, or—"

"Eating or sleeping," her husband chuckled. "Come, find the policeman some food. He has far to travel."

124

As he lay there listening, pretending to sleep, Johani's heart was filled with anxiety. He learned that there were seven extra policemen patrolling the snow-covered country north of Niklander's settlement, making nine when Sergeant Peaksi and his regular constable were counted. Not one Lapp family had been overlooked, and each had received a solemn warning of what would happen to them if they gave aid to the wanted Sarris family.

"We are fairly certain where they are now," the policeman confided. "Sergeant Peaksi is a clever man. He has worked out on the map the one place where they can be."

"Oh, and where is that?" Pekka Aikio asked, cracking the shinbone of a reindeer and sucking the marrow from it with noisy relish.

"In the Loktajaurre!" the policeman said, and half turned as he heard Johani's stifled gasp.

"Somebody dreaming," Mother Aikio chuckled, reaching for the policeman's cup and diverting his attention.

"Yes, in the Loktajaurre," the policeman went on, "and Sergeant Peaksi is only waiting for a good weather report from the meteorologists . . ."

"From the who?" Pekka asked, mystified.

"The meteorologists," the policeman said, and gave a self-satisfied laugh. "You may think you understand the weather, Pekka Aikio, but the meteorologists can tell days ahead whether it is going to be stormy, snowy, or clear. Just as soon as they say it will be fine for a day or so, Sergeant Peaksi will fly in again with the helicopter, and he won't just have a few forest Lapps with him this time. That will be the end of the Sarris family."

"And a good thing too," Pekka grunted. "It disturbs us

125

to have policemen coming here every few days. Not," he added hurriedly, "that we do not like to have policemen visiting; it is simply that our herdsmen are anxious to win this reward of ten reindeer, and they keep straying away from their own work to look for the Sarris herd."

"They'll have to be quick if they want to win anything now," the policeman said. "You said there was going to be some fine weather, didn't you?"

"Any day now the skies should clear. Then we will have a few days of quiet," Pekka agreed. "Sometimes it lasts a week."

"That will be long enough for Sergeant Peaksi," the policeman said, and offered Pekka a cigarette.

After more talk and a final drink of coffee the policeman left the tent. There was a minute or so of commotion outside while his reindeer ox was harnessed to his sleigh —he did not use a Lapp *pulka;* then he was off, with only one more Lapp family to visit before he returned to make his report at Niklander's settlement.

Pekka came back into the tent and closed the flap. "Well, Johani Sarris," he said, "if you have not been sleeping, you will know what is going to happen, eh?"

"What can we do?" Johani asked, sitting up. "I came here to ask for food and reindeer moss for the herd. Unless we get moss, there will be starvation in the Loktajaurre."

Pekka shook his head slowly. "No one is to give, lend, or sell anything to the Sarris family. In any case, when the weather clears Sergeant Peaksi will fly in that noisy red thing, and he will be in the Loktajaurre in an hour or so. It may be difficult for an Outlander on skis to find his way, but the flying machine takes no heed of bad passes and deep snow. So . . . !" And he shrugged.

Johani sat with his shoulders slumped until Mother Aikio laid a hand on them and said, a twinkle in her eyes, "When Pekka and I lie down, there is no reason at all why you should not help yourself to coffee, sugar, flour, salt—anything you need. You know that if a man is out on the hills, hungry, maybe lost, no one is angry if he kills a reindeer belonging to another man. It is the custom."

Johani looked at her, and somehow he had to smile. Her dark, twinkling eyes reminded him of his mother, who never gave way to despair.

"Thank you," he began, only to be cut short by Pekka, who said with mock sternness, "No, you cannot thank us, for we are not allowed to give—*give*, mind you—anything. You will have stolen the coffee, sugar, salt, flour—do not forget that. I would give you nothing. My fat wife would give you nothing. Mother, make sure he knows where everything is before we lie down to sleep."

Johani smiled his thanks, but he was still desperately anxious. "It is reindeer moss I need most."

"I can give you no moss," Pekka said. "Why should I feed a herd which will surely be taken down to Niklander's settlement? What I can do is take your reindeer until the spring comes."

"Take the . . . ?" Johani stared, not quite grasping the offer being made.

"Keep your herd with you, Johani Sarris, and as sure as I am now filling my pipe with tobacco, Sergeant Peaksi will take it from you. He has extra policemen; he has the flying machine. You cannot live much longer in the Loktajaurre. He will find you, take you south, take the herd south and give it to butcher Nillson unless . . ."

"Unless?"

"Unless your beasts are swallowed up in my herd," Pekka chuckled. "I have more than a thousand reindeer. Add your three or four hundred to them and who would know they are there, except my herders? And they will not talk."

"Would you?" Johani could hardly believe this good luck.

"You must come for them in the spring," Pekka warned. "While the sun is away no one will find out what has happened; but when the days grow light, and the sun stays longer and longer, then even a policeman will recognize the ear-clips of the Sarris family."

"That won't matter," Johani said joyfully. "When spring is here my father will have returned, and he will be able to prove to the policeman that he did not sell the herd."

Pekka and his fat, jolly wife lay down, and chuckled as Johani filled small sacks with coffee, sugar, salt, and flour. He took them out and loaded them into his *pulka*.

Two nights later, under a clear starry sky, the Sarris herd came over the snow-covered hills. No bell *tong-tonged*, for Johani was afraid of meeting a wandering policeman.

Pekka and his eldest son took charge of the Sarris herd, and drove them in fifties to the various feeding grounds. Pekka was a wealthy man, and there were many *pulka*-loads of reindeer moss to eke out the grazing, so the Sarris reindeer were allowed to eat their fill before they joined the various herds.

Johani, Anna, and even Mikkel were loud in their thanks to Pekka and his wife. When they had gone, however, Pekka sat gnawing the end of his unlit pipe.

128

"What is the matter now?" his wife asked, between chewing on reindeer sinews from which she would get threads for mending *skaller* or torn reindeer robes. "You look as if you had swallowed too much meat and it lay heavy as lead in your belly!"

"I know something I did not tell the Sarris children," Pekka muttered. "I asked the policeman who came last if there was news of Jouni Sarris. I asked how his burns were mending."

"And what did he tell you?" his wife asked anxiously.

"They are mending," Pekka said, "but slowly. Jouni will not be back here when spring returns. He will not be back until it is summer."

"Well, if he comes back healthy, that is good," his wife said.

"Sometimes I think women see no further than the length of a reindeer's tail," Pekka grumbled. "I dare not keep the Sarris reindeer after spring comes. By then this policeman Peaksi will be searching once more for them. He knows a herd does not vanish like snow in summer. Johani and Anna will be caught, and Jouni will not be there to prove he did not sell his herd to the Swedish butcher."

"Perhaps Jouni will get better more quickly than the Outlander doctors think, and return before spring," his wife suggested.

"Perhaps the sun will be high in the sky tomorrow," Pekka said tartly. "Wife, the doctors say *late summer*—too late to help the Sarris children."

II

River in Flood

Johani, Anna, and Mikkel kept five reindeer, two to haul the *pulkas* and three to be slaughtered for food. Their dogs they had left with Pekka and his wife.

The lack of dogs almost proved disastrous, for it was a hard winter and the wolves were desperate for food. They mauled one reindeer so badly that it had to be killed. But Johani, in a desperate effort to save it, did manage to kill two of the attackers. They were skinned and their hides taken to Bossekop by Mikkel, who kept his face hidden as much as possible so that no one would recognize him. There he exchanged the hides for fresh supplies of sugar, coffee, and flour, and got all the latest gossip.

Sergeant Peaksi had visited the Loktajaurre valley and, finding no herd, had given up the search for the time being. Wherever Lapps met they discussed the herd that had vanished. The older Lapps said that Stallo had swallowed it and the Sarris children. Stallo was a Lapp demon with a huge mouth and great teeth. He was supposed to lie in wait by a rock for some unwary traveler to pass by. When the traveler vanished, gulped down by Stallo, the demon left a rock in his place.

The younger Lapps scoffed at the story of Stallo, but no one could explain where the Sarris herd had gone, or even where Johani and Anna were. Some said they must have gone east into Russia.

Then one day, when Johani was lying on a frozen lake, fishing through a hole he had cut in the ice, he noticed a suggestion of color on the windswept surface.

Raising himself on one elbow, he looked back and immediately forgot about fishing. Down on the southeastern horizon a thin red line was showing. It was not a fire; it could not be the northern lights. There was only one thing it could be, and Johani's heart raced with joy at the thought—it was the sun!

The red line grew thicker, changed color slowly until it was shimmering gold, then began to fade again. Sunrise and sunset both occurred in a single hour, but it was wonderful news to take back to Anna and Mikkel.

The weeks which followed brought snow, bitter cold, but always a little more daylight. Sometimes, when the sky had cleared after a storm, the three of them would see the whole of the blood-red ball which was the sun. Sometimes they could even feel its warmth, and occasionally there would be tiny drips of water from icicles.

The woods of dwarf birch, silent for so long, started to come to life again. The tits and Siberian jays, which had hung about the Sarris tent throughout the blackest days, moved off. The jays, which had been bleak-eyed and silent, began to whistle tunefully. Flocks of snow sparrows appeared, a sign that the snow was beginning to melt.

The days lengthened quickly, and soon dawn was ushered in by the harsh cry of the ptarmigan, a stuttering machine-gun fire of *kopek-kopek-kopek-kopek-pek-pek-pek—peh—pek.*

Blackcocks appeared, then the capercailzies could be heard clappering and sharpening their beaks, their plumage bright and glossy.

February, March, and the first week of April came and went, and patches of bare ground began to show. The ice was cracking on the rivers. One day, as if it were a date they had agreed on, Johani, Anna, and Mikkel made ready to move. They packed their tent, harnessed the two reindeer they had left, and struck out for the tents of Pekka Aikio and his wife.

Pekka was delighted to see them, and very anxious to hand over the Sarris reindeer. He had already had them picked out from among the others and kept on their own.

"I had to do this, Johani," he said, "for that wolverine of a policeman has been here—Sergeant Peaksi. He—"

"Did he have any news of my father?" Johani interrupted.

"Yes. Jouni is getting better, but very slowly. They have told him nothing of what is going on. The doctors refuse to let the police question him because they are afraid bad news might cause a setback. And what could he do, anyway? He might say he did not sell the herd, but that swindling Gustav has the contract, and it is also signed by Paavo Niklander whom everybody trusts."

Pekka shook his head dolefully, then clapped a hand

on Johani's shoulder. "You must get on your way quickly, my boy. The policemen have gone north. They know the herds will soon be moving up into the higher hills and they mean to come down slowly, examining every herd that comes along. They know the valleys along which the herds travel, so you must hurry. Try to get over into Russia if you can. It is your only chance."

Thanking him for all he had done, Johani and Anna offered reindeer as payment for the help they had received from the Aikio family.

"There is not a Lapp family in the hills who would not have done something to help, Johani," Pekka assured him. "We all think there has been a trick somewhere. Your father would never sell his herd, as I told the policeman. Now go—and some time, when I am an old man, you can buy me a new pipe and a packet of tobacco."

Pekka's thousand head of reindeer were on the move north within an hour after the Sarris herd had climbed the hill into the next valley. Pekka's dogs were yapping joyfully, the children shouting, for they all loved this time of the year. But there was no shouting around the Sarris herd. In these vast, silent hills and valleys sounds carried far, and Johani, Anna, and Mikkel were afraid that they might be heard or seen by some lynx-eyed policeman lying in wait for them.

Two days they journeyed northeast, with the surface of the snow crisp after frost at night. Then came a period of thirty-six hours when the dreaded *sose*, or thaw, softened the snow. Rain clouds swirled over the hilltops, and there was the rippling sound of running water as the streams finally broke free from the ice.

A night of frost hardened the surface again and, with every single one of the herd anxious to get north, they moved on once more. Two days later, they had just finished congratulating each other on the progress they were making when the sun twinkled for a few moments on something ahead. The man with the binoculars did not realize that the sun on his lens had given him away, but the keen eyes of Mikkel, who first saw the twinkling shimmer of light, made out the tiny figure.

The herd was turned due east now, but the damage had been done. The policeman sped away and soon made contact with Sergeant Peaksi. He and his men could travel even faster than the quick-moving herd, and for much longer periods, snatching a meal from their packs with only the shortest of halts.

Spring was coming in earnest now, for it was almost May, and as if to make up for the previous year's bad summer, the sun was shining with ever growing strength. Larger and larger patches of gray-green moss were revealed daily as the snow melted away. The air was filled with the sound of rushing water. Rivers were running high, and their currents were so strong that Mikkel advised getting the herd together and making the crossings in as close a mass as possible.

They entered a long valley which rose slowly to a height of three thousand feet. On either side were steep hills, black where the rock was free from snow and ice, white where the stones still held the snow.

"Another two days, Johani, and we shall be in Russia," Mikkel announced gleefully.

Johani merely nodded. For some reason he could not explain, he had been growing more and more uneasy.

134

He kept looking back, half fearing to see men following them, and later that day his fears were realized.

The herd had been halted on a patch of reindeer moss and was feeding with zest. Anna had lit a fire and the men were waiting for her to call them to eat. From the top of the hillside Johani's gaze strayed back down the valley. He stared, wiped his eyes with the back of his glove to make sure they were clear, then looked again. His heart sank, for there was no doubt about it; the two black spots he could see were men. At this time of the year Lapp men always traveled with their herds, so he was sure these two must be policemen.

Anna hurriedly took her pan of stew from the fire and stood it in a bank of snow to cool. If it thickened, it could be carried on the *pulka* without spilling and eaten later. Johani and Mikkel called the dogs, and forced the reluctant herd to leave its browsing and move once more.

The black dots grew slowly larger as the two policemen reduced the distance which separated them from their quarry. Sergeant Peaksi and his constable were tired, for they had been traveling almost continuously, yet sight of the herd which had "vanished" so mysteriously at the beginning of the winter made them more determined than ever to reach the Sarris family.

Over the rise at the head of the long valley and down into the next one went the herd. It had gone a mile in the new valley and was trotting along at a good speed, when the comforting *tong-tong* of the leader's bell faltered and then ceased. The steady *clack-clack-clackety-clack* of hoofs also faltered, and the bulk of the animals closed in around the leaders. Johani and Mikkel raced along each side of the herd to see what was holding it up.

In silent consternation Johani halted at the fringe of a flooded river. Here, where the upland valley narrowed, the water formed a barrier. It flowed from the snout of a glacier on the north side and turned only when it broke into foam against a rearing black wall of rock. From there it plunged east down a boulder-strewn bed, noisy and white with upflung spray.

In summer it would be a fast-flowing stream of perhaps forty yards' width. Now, with the sun melting snow everywhere, the river was more like eighty yards wide and was a brown, racing flood with a smooth-looking surface. This was a bad sign, for a shallow stream almost always has a broken surface, since stones on the bottom make ripples. When a river is in flood and the surface looks smooth, it is a sure sign of deep water.

Mikkel splashed along the shallows where the river had spread beyond its natural banks, and looked glumly at Johani.

"If we could only wait until early morning," the old man said, "the water level would probably have fallen as much as the distance from a man's elbow to his wrist. Once the sun goes down, the snow ceases to melt and there is less water."

"Go back and ask the policemen if they will wait," Johani suggested, a grim little smile on his face. "This is just what they've been hoping for. We've got to cross now if we're to cross at all. Here we win or lose."

Mikkel nodded, then he and Johani prepared to stake everything on a crossing. Hand in hand, each steadying himself with his ski stick, they struggled to midstream. A man on his own could not have survived, for the racing water plucked at them with tremendous force. To make matters worse, the stream bed was very rough: stones rolled under their feet.

Beyond, like the Promised Land, the valley sloped down to broader stretches of gray-green which could only mean patches of rich reindeer moss. Once they were safely across, the herd could browse on this lichen for an hour or so, then trot on toward the Finnish-Russian frontier and safety from Sergeant Peaksi and his constable. As Johani had said, it was win everything or lose everything.

Knotting their lassos together gave the two men enough line to span the flooded river. They hauled one laden *pulka* across, and then Anna came with the second *pulka*. The thin black length of lasso line twanged and jerked under the strain, but it held.

"You stay here," Johani said to Mikkel and Anna. "I'll get the herd moving in as solid a bunch as possible. If they can keep together, they'll hold one another up in the water."

With a lasso tied about his waist in case he lost his footing, Johani went back across the raging river. It was a grim struggle, and sometimes the water was up to his armpits as he bent to keep his balance. The current was like some hungry animal clawing at him, and the stones moved constantly under his feet. When he joined the herd once more, he was gasping for breath.

Johani released the lasso loop from his waist and Mikkel hauled the knotted lines back, untied them, and coiled them. His own lasso he slipped across one shoulder, ready for use in an emergency. The second he looped over a rock, calling Johani's attention to it so that he

137

would not forget it. The lasso, to a Lapp herdsman, is like a third hand.

With the dogs helping, Johani got the first of the reindeer into the shallows. They probably would have drawn back at the hidden bank where the water suddenly grew deeper by nearly two feet, but the press of animals crowding behind prevented them from doing so. Nostrils dilated, eyes wide, and heads thrown back, the first few reindeer could do nothing but plunge on. The current caught them, and they were swept yards downstream before some managed to get their feet on the bottom while others started to swim.

When the main body of the herd got into the water, the task of crossing was easier. As Johani had prophesied, the reindeer kept one another upright. But one yearling cow in the first bunch was swept farther downstream than the others. It struck out boldly for the shore, but was still yards from safety when it reached the point where the flood hit the black wall of rock. In an instant it was swept away and lost in a welter of boiling foam.

Johani became desperate. A dozen reindeer were still milling about on the edge of the stream, and Sergeant Peaksi and his constable were now little more than a hundred yards away. Yelling to his dogs, Johani made a rush at the frightened animals who remained, shouting and waving his arms.

One reindeer panicked and splashed into the water. The others followed, except for one big bull which turned for a moment or so and held the dogs at bay. Johani bellowed at it. The bull held its ground for a second, then lost its nerve. It bolted for the river, and a tremendous leap carried it yards from the bank. For several seconds it was lost from view in a great surge of water.

Johani followed it in, for Sergeant Peaksi was very close now. But the dogs were too cunning to try a straight-across swim. They raced upstream, knowing the current would sweep them down, no matter how hard they fought it.

In the next few seconds all seemed to be going well. Johani was moving cautiously across the stream, shivering at the iciness of the water, and the big bull was swimming strongly, even though he was being swept slightly downstream.

The other reindeer had scrambled ashore and the bull was now within a few yards of the bank, where old Mikkel was waiting, gently swinging his lasso loop, ready to drop it over the animal's head if help were needed.

Then, for some reason, the bull changed direction and turned downstream. At once the current swept it on at racing speed, and less than eighty yards away the river was boiling into foam where the rushing water hurled itself against the foot of the cliff.

Old Mikkel reacted immediately. He swung his lasso and the loop snaked out to settle neatly over the bull's head. The old man braced himself to take the shock, but he had misjudged the strength of the current. Johani, who had just regained his balance after slipping on a loose stone underfoot, looked up in time to see the disaster. Mikkel's rope tightened as the big bull swept by, but instead of checking the animal's headlong rush, the old man himself was jerked into the river. For a moment he seemed to hover in the air, arms flailing, then there was a splash and he was lost to sight.

Johani could do nothing, and Anna was some distance away down the valley. As the young Lapp struggled to get to the bank he saw one of Mikkel's arms break the

surface for a second, only to be lost again in the brown
flood.

The bull reached the bank downstream and began to
scramble out of the water. Johani, too, felt the first
sloping of the bank under his feet, and fought harder to
get ashore. Meanwhile, the bull's progress had been
halted by the rope about its neck. The rope was taut as a
fiddlestring, for Mikkel had tied the free end of the
lasso to his wrist, and now it was holding him like a
hooked fish.

Johani struggled up the bank. Half choked, the reindeer bull had ceased to move. The lasso loop was draw-

ing tighter and tighter around its throat, cutting off its air supply. The animal was slowly being strangled to death. If it collapsed, it would slide down the slippery bank and the current would sweep both it and Mikkel away in a matter of seconds.

Exhausted, gulping for breath, Johani finally reached the top of the bank. He needed air, he needed to rest; yet he dared not stop for either. Old Mikkel, face down in the water, would be dead within a minute if the reindeer lost his battle with the rope.

Somehow Johani reached the bull. Digging in his heels, he pulled on the taut lasso. The gasping bull tottered half a pace forward, its legs shaking, its flanks heaving spasmodically as it tried to breathe.

Johani gave another hard pull. Like a stranded fish, Mikkel was drawn into the shallows. He was still face down, still in some nine inches of water. Johani felt dizzy, but he pulled again. Mikkel was dragged clear and lay halfway up the bank, water draining from his sodden clothing. Johani slid down to him with his last bit of strength. Mikkel looked dead, and Johani did not know how to help him.

From the opposite bank Sergeant Peaksi and his constable had been in time to watch the last few moments of the drama. The constable shook his head dubiously. "Too risky," he muttered, hoping Sergeant Peaksi would agree with him. "We can't cross here."

"If we hold on to each other, we can," was the sergeant's crisp retort. "Come on! These Lapps don't know the first thing about artificial respiration. While we stand here watching, the old man may be dying. Give me your arm, and don't let go, no matter what happens!"

12

Sergeant Peaksi Triumphs

"There's something else besides saving the old man," Sergeant Peaksi said as he stepped into the fringe of the flood. "If we can get across now, we can arrest the three of them and make them bring their herd back. That's what we're here for, my friend, and don't forget it."

"Yes," the constable spluttered as he followed barely half a pace behind Peaksi, gasping as the icy water reached up his legs, past his knees, and almost to his thighs. "We'll . . . kill more than . . . two birds . . . with one . . . stone, Sergeant. If we're . . . not lucky . . . we'll . . . kill ourselves."

Sergeant Peaksi went on without a word, taking risks he would not usually have taken. He struggled up the far bank and hurried over to Johani, who was trying to up-end the unconscious Mikkel—the only way he could think of to empty the water from the old man's lungs.

The sergeant and his constable brushed Johani aside,

and the two policemen bent to the task of applying the latest method of resuscitation. In ten minutes Mikkel was breathing again—feebly, but the blueness was going from his lips.

"Now, some warm clothing, Sarris," Sergeant Peaksi ordered. "Hurry! or he will die from shock and exposure." When Johani moved away, the sergeant winked knowingly at his constable and murmured, "That'll get the girl here as well."

"There's something more than just shock wrong with this man," the constable muttered. "He shouldn't be lying like this. Listen to his breathing."

"He probably took a bad blow on his head," Peaksi said. "May be suffering from concussion. Anyway, when Sarris comes back, leave the talking to me. If we play our cards right, we'll save Mikkel *and* get the herd back to the settlement without too much trouble. We could never do it alone."

"If we'd arrested them we—"

"You still have a lot to learn about Lapps and reindeer," Sergeant Peaksi interrupted grimly. "Suppose we did arrest Sarris and his sister. What would we do with the reindeer? Have you thought of that?"

"We'd make the Lapps drive the herd back to the settlement."

Sergeant Peaksi laughed scornfully. "And I suppose we could make water run uphill, too? All winter we've been trying to find Sarris, his sister, the old man here, and their reindeer."

"Yes, but it's different now," the constable said. "The days are light and—"

"Yes, the days are light," Sergeant Peaksi agreed mock-

143

ingly, "and the reindeer calves are being born. The mosquitoes are starting to appear, too. Know what that means? When the mosquitoes come, the reindeer go— up to the hilltops as fast as they can, away from the pests. We want to drive the herd south of here, but they'll head north if they can. It'll need all the skill and patience of the Sarris family to get that herd down to the settlement, and if we can't persuade them to do it willingly, I know we can't force them."

"I don't know much about Lapps," the constable confessed, "but it seems to me if you pointed out that we represent the law and . . ." He stopped as Sergeant Peaksi burst out laughing.

"They've managed a long time without policemen, my lad, and they're a peaceful people. They have their own laws, and they've got along quite well without us; why should they worry about laws made in Finland? Anyway, I've got an idea I can persuade them to help, so you keep your tongue between your teeth and leave all the talking to me."

When Johani came back with a laden *pulka* drawn by a very reluctant reindeer ox, and an even more reluctant Anna following behind, Sergeant Peaksi was ready.

"Get a fire going, and give me robes and a sleeping bag to keep the old man warm. It's going to be a case of touch-and-go whether he will live."

"Will he want food?" Anna asked, looking down in alarm at Mikkel's face, now beginning to show bruises where he had been struck by rocks during his passage through the water.

"Not yet," the sergeant said. "Warmth. That's what's

144

essential now. He won't regain consciousness for some time, so he won't be able to swallow anything, not even soup."

While Anna lit a fire, Johani prepared a sleeping bag and got out a fur *peske*. The sergeant stripped Mikkel of his sodden clothing, and he and the constable rubbed him until his skin was rough and red. Then they wrapped him in one of the *peskes,* robes used during the very worst cold weather of the winter. Looking like a cocoon, he was then eased into a sleeping bag.

Sergeant Peaksi was satisfied that Mikkel was warm enough, but his face was grave as he felt the old man's pulse. It was slow and rather shallow.

He made Johani feel the pulse, too. "What do you make of that, Sarris?" he asked.

Johani looked puzzled. He knew nothing about pulse beats; but when the sergeant showed him how to feel his own wrist pulse and count, then do the same with Mikkel, he realized the difference.

"What does it mean?" he asked.

"He's got to be taken to the hospital, to a doctor," the sergeant said. "If he doesn't get to one soon—well . . ." His shrug suggested that the old man would surely die.

Johani looked blankly at the sergeant, then cast a swift glance toward his sister and asked, "Could I go for the flying machine? I did it once before when my father was burned."

Sergeant Peaksi slowly shook his head before saying, "No, Sarris. If you did, there would be no one to keep the reindeer herd together. Besides, I am here to arrest you and Mikkel, and you know the reason why."

Johani stared, gulped, then protested, "But Mikkel

will die! You said if he did not reach a doctor he would—"

"The constable and I can get him to a doctor," Sergeant Peaksi said quietly, "if you promise me something."

"Yes, I will promise," Johani said quickly. "Mikkel is a friend—almost like one of the Sarris family. He has been with us since I was a very small boy. What do you want me to do?"

"You'd better come and listen to this," Sergeant Peaksi said, looking across at Anna. "It concerns you as much as your brother." He cleared his throat, then said quietly, deliberately, laying emphasis on practically every word:

"I have been sent out here by the sheriff to bring you and the Sarris herd down to Niklander's settlement. The trader is waiting for the herd. He bought it—three hundred head of reindeer. You know who I mean; Mr. Gustav Nillson. He is demanding the reindeer for which he paid a lot of money."

"But my father would never sell so many reindeer," Johani broke in passionately. "I know he would not."

"You've said that before," Sergeant Peaksi said coolly, "but the point is that Mr. Nillson has a paper which proves he bought and paid for the reindeer. Now, I am here to see that the herd goes back. I can take your friend Mikkel to the doctor, but on one condition only."

He paused and looked from Johani to Anna as if he expected them to guess what he was going to say. But their wind-and-weather-darkened faces gave no sign that they knew what was in store for them. Sergeant Peaksi went on quietly: "I will see that Mikkel reaches a doctor within the next four or five days. You will stay here, round up the reindeer, then start bringing the herd into the settlement. I shall give you fourteen days to do it, for

146

I know it is time for the calves to be born and that the herd will want to go north, not south. But if I save Mikkel, you must bring the Sarris herd to Niklander's settlement."

Johani's mouth opened; he gulped, gulped again, then looked miserably at Anna. Anna dropped to one knee and began pleading with Mikkel to speak to her. But the old man continued to lie motionless and breathed in heavy snores—a sure sign that he was suffering from concussion.

"I am sorry," Sergeant Peaksi said finally, laying a hand gently on her shoulder. "He will not hear you."

When the sergeant turned from Anna, it was to face a Johani who looked much older than sixteen.

"There is no other way to save Mikkel than this?" Johani asked. "It will mean losing the Sarris reindeer, and they were put in my charge when our father was taken away."

Sergeant Peaksi had to force himself to be stern. He reminded himself that he had a duty to do, and said soberly, "I am sorry, Sarris, but the sheriff has ordered that you and the herd shall be brought in. I dare not return to Niklander's settlement without them, even if I take Mikkel in, unless I can say that you have promised to bring in your herd and your sister."

Johani nodded. "Take Mikkel," he said heavily. "The Sarris herd will be at the settlement within fourteen days."

After sunset the air grew colder and the flow of water from beneath the glacier almost stopped. The snow, still dappling the side of the valley in patches, took on a crisp surface again and ceased to melt. As a result there was much less water draining into the river; the flood level dropped and the roar became a murmur. Sergeant Peaksi, his constable, Anna, and Johani each took a corner of the *pulka* on which they had strapped Mikkel, and got the old man across the river without incident.

The strongest reindeer ox was put in the *pulka* harness, with a spare ox as a relief. Mikkel was wrapped in two fur *peskes* to ensure warmth and keep him as free from jolts as possible.

Before they parted, Sergeant Peaksi looked at Johani and said quietly, "I am trusting you. If you do not follow me with the herd, I shall be ruined, perhaps dismissed from the police."

"The herd will reach Niklander's settlement within fourteen days," Johani said. "I hope you and the constable get Mikkel to the doctor in time, that is all."

The *pulka* moved west, and not until police, reindeer oxen, and *pulka* had faded to the merest speck did Anna cry. She turned to stare down the valley where the Sarris herd was grazing happily on the great carpet of reindeer moss, then tears welled up in her eyes and ran unchecked down her wind-tanned cheeks.

Johani had never seen his sister cry before, and he did not know what to do or say. Miserably he walked down the gentle slope, and as he neared the first patch of snow he saw something struggle upright. A cow had just given birth to a calf and was nuzzling it now, trying to persuade the baby to get to its feet. It was a scene Johani had witnessed many times before, but he stood and watched in silence.

The cow finally succeeded, and the youngster stood for

a moment on its shaky, rubbery-looking legs. Then one leg betrayed it and the calf flopped back onto the snow. The reindeer cow lowed encouragingly and the calf tried again. It rose, then fell, rose, lasted a few moments on its unsteady legs, then flopped once more.

Johani watched in frowning silence as the calf tried time after time to stand. Its mother seemed puzzled that her baby should be such a stupid thing as not to be able to walk. Finally, however, the rubbery legs gained strength, and as the reindeer moved away, the calf followed, slowly, unsteadily. It was then that Johani's eyes lit up.

Turning, he sped back up the valley to where Anna was sitting on a rock, her hands about her knees. She was staring miserably toward the northeast where the sky was beginning to show the first yellow patches of the new sun, even though it was hardly three o'clock in the morning.

"Anna," Johani said, smiling. "It won't be the end for us when we get back to Niklander's settlement. There is no need to cry. We *shall* have a herd for the time when Father and Mother return to the hills."

"Who will give us reindeer?" Anna asked suspiciously.

"There is no need for anyone to *give* us anything," Johani said joyfully. "Is this not calving time? I have just seen the first of our new herd born. By the time we get to Niklander's place and meet this thieving trader we shall have many calves. Don't you see, by keeping the herd through the winter we have won for ourselves a new herd?"

Anna pondered, then shook her head. "Will the calves not belong to Mr. Nillson?" she asked.

"No," said Johani firmly. "This paper the police talk of so much says that he bought three hundred reindeer. Very well, we can let him have just three hundred—but the calves belong to us!"

"How many calves?" Anna whispered. "Last spring was a bad one and many were lost."

"None will be lost this time," Johani assured her. "You will see. Now come, let us go and count."

By the time they were ready to start moving southwest toward Niklander's settlement, sixty-seven calves had been born and only one had died. When they rested at the bottom of the Narrow Valley, almost at the spot where they had tussled with Sergeant Peaksi and the four forest Lapps, nine more calves were born.

It was there they received a shock. Down the Narrow Valley came a policeman and two Lapps with dogs. Johani and Anna stared at the herdsmen, for the men did not wear the Four Winds cap which the Finnish Lapps wore. Instead their caps were adorned with a fancy red pompon.

"They are from across the border," Anna said, suddenly remembering that once when she was a small child she had gone to Bossekop, and there had seen men wearing these same red decorations.

"Swedish Lapps," Johani muttered, and was uneasy; Gustav Nillson was Swedish, too. He and Anna waited in some fear as the policeman drew nearer.

The two Lapps called their dogs to heel, and Johani did the same with his, which were prowling around and snarling, their hackles up, ready to do battle with the strangers.

The policeman was the same man who had been with

Sergeant Peaksi at the river. "I have been sent by the sheriff to bring you in," he said.

"We shall be moving the herd tomorrow," Johani answered. "There are still two days left of the fourteen the sergeant said he would allow me."

"Yes, I know," the policeman said briskly, "but the sheriff is at Niklander's settlement, and in a bad temper. Mr. Nillson has been making trouble over the reindeer, and he wants to get them away to Sweden as soon as possible. That is why these two herdsmen are here now. They will bring the herd in to the settlement, but you and your sister are to come with me now. The case will be tried just as soon as you get there."

"Case!" Johani and Anna were puzzled by the word. "What is a case?"

The policeman sighed. There were so many things these hill Lapps did not understand.

"You stole Mr. Gustav Nillson's reindeer," he said. "You refused to bring them back, even when Sergeant Peaksi spoke to you. You have kept them hidden all through the winter. So you will have to be punished."

Johani tried to argue, but the policeman would not listen.

"You just come with me. If you can persuade the sheriff that you did not run away with the Swede's reindeer, good luck to you. These Swedish Lapps will look after the herd. They're going to drive the reindeer across the border as soon as the court has decided your case. Come on, now."

13

A *Surprising* Verdict

The court was the large room in the rebuilt house which had once belonged to Paavo Niklander. Everybody from the settlement who could crowd into the room had done so. Gustav Nillson was there too, and he frowned whenever he looked across at Johani and Anna.

They were sitting together on a bench, confused by the strangeness and solemnity of the proceedings, and frightened at the thought of what might happen to them. But they were happy about one thing: Mikkel was recovering. Sergeant Peaksi had gotten him to the doctor in time, and the sturdy old herdsman was already up and about.

The sheriff sat behind a table, on top of which were a book and some papers, as well as a pen and a bottle of ink. Sergeant Peaksi seemed to be in charge, and when he lifted a hand for silence the chattering of the crowd died down.

Everything had to be simple, so that not only Johani and Anna could understand, but also the people from the settlement. It was from them that visiting Lapps would get the news of what happened to people like Johani and Anna Sarris who broke the law and even defied officials like Sergeant Peaksi.

Sergeant Peaksi read out the charge, that Johani Sarris, aided by his sister Anna and their herdsman Mikkel, had assaulted a policeman guarding reindeer purchased by a Swedish trader, Gustav Nillson by name. He had taken away the reindeer, later hiding them somewhere to the north, so that Mr. Gustav Nillson had not been able to supply his customers, and had thereby lost a considerable sum of money.

It seemed as if the sheriff, a big man with a gray moustache, was in a hurry, for without wasting a moment he turned and, pointing his pen at Johani, asked: "Did you lasso a policeman guarding reindeer in a corral out there?" He pointed in the direction of the corrals.

"Yes, but there—"

"Did you take away more than three hundred head of reindeer?" the sheriff interrupted. "Yes or no?"

"Yes, but my father—"

"Did you later take the same reindeer from the care of Sergeant Peaksi and four forest Lapp herdsmen?"

Johani drew a deep breath and nodded.

"Yes or no. People cannot hear a nod of the head," the sheriff said.

"Yes," Johani said defiantly.

"Right. Now, Mr. Gustav Nillson. You are a trader; you come to this settlement year after year to buy reindeer, many of which are slaughtered here and then taken

153

by sledge across to your own country. Is that correct?"

"Yes, Sheriff."

"You were having difficulty in buying reindeer last round-up, because it had been a bad year for the Lapps. So you persuaded a man named Jouni Sarris to sell you three hundred of his small herd."

"Yes, and I paid for them in the—"

"I shall ask the questions," the sheriff snapped. "Now, you had the usual agreement, which Jouni Sarris witnessed by putting a cross against his name. Mr. Paavo Niklander, who at that time owned this store, was also a witness. He signed the agreement as well as yourself?"

"Yes, Sheriff."

"He saw you hand over the money?"

"Yes."

A paper was passed across to Gustav Nillson, and he was asked if that was the agreement by which he had bought the three hundred Sarris reindeer. Nillson looked at the paper, nodded, and passing the paper back said, "That is the paper, Sheriff."

The sheriff turned and again wagged his pen at Johani.

"Now, are you convinced that your father sold three hundred reindeer to Mr. Nillson?"

Johani shook his head stubbornly. "My father would be a fool to do such a thing—and the Sarris men have never been fools."

There were chuckles from the men sitting on the benches against the wall, but they died down when the sheriff tapped the table with the end of his pen and in a quiet voice said, "Johani is quite right when he says the Sarris men are not fools, for Jouni Sarris *did not sell* three hundred of his herd." He paused for a moment, then

154

looked across at the astonished face of Gustav Nillson. A gasp went up from the audience, and Johani and Anna exchanged startled glances, as though neither of them could believe what had just been said.

There was anger in the sheriff's voice as he continued: "Mr. Nillson, I have not worked among the Lapps as long as I have without learning something about them. You had a signed contract of sale, but I was far from satisfied. At first Jouni Sarris was too ill to be able to tell the police anything. His wife Kirsti was sure her husband would never sell so many reindeer—but words mean little against a contract which is signed and witnessed. There was nothing we could do at that time but order the arrest of Johani for taking the herd away."

He stopped, and for a few moments there was silence in the crowded room, broken only by the tapping of the sheriff's pen on the table. At last he started speaking again: "Then we learned that Mr. Niklander had left the district soon after the disastrous fire and returned to Finland where he started a small business. We thought that was rather odd, for when we made inquiries we discovered that his house and store up here had not been insured. We decided to find out where he had obtained money for a new business, and . . ."

"I protest, Sheriff," Gustav Nillson began. "I had my signed contract, and . . ." A long hard stare from the sheriff silenced him before he could say more.

"I have some interesting news for you, Mr. Nillson," the sheriff said. The room was now breathlessly quiet. "The police questioned Paavo Niklander as to where he got the money to start a new business, and he finally told them. He confessed that you had persuaded him to alter

155

the contract so that it showed Jouni Sarris to have sold not thirty reindeer, but three hundred. A zero added to thirty was easy. Another zero added to the amount of money supposed to have been handed over to Jouni Sarris was just as easy to add. I . . ."

"It's a lie," Nillson shouted, his face contorted with rage, "and I can . . ."

"Sit down or I will have you handcuffed and taken outside," the sheriff said coldly. Then he gave a signal to the constable standing by the door, who ushered into the room a pale-faced Paavo Niklander.

In a strained voice Niklander told how Gustav Nillson

had persuaded him to take part in the plot to cheat Jouni Sarris, how he had later witnessed the altered contract and then swore to the police that Jouni had actually agreed to sell, and been paid for, three hundred head of reindeer.

When Niklander had finished, he was led from the room along with Nillson; both of them would be sentenced by a higher court in Finland itself.

All the Lapps in the audience were smiling now, and Johani embraced Anna in a proud hug.

The sheriff leaned his elbows on the table, and after stroking his big gray moustache for a few moments, he wagged a finger at the happy onlookers. "Sometimes you people think the sheriff and the police are here only to make sure you pay your taxes. In the case of Jouni and his reindeer, I suppose we would not have been able to do anything if young Johani had not taken the law into his own hands and spirited the herd away. But still Johani did break the law, and anyone who does that must be punished."

The smiles faded from the faces of the listening Lapps. Surely the sheriff was joking, they thought.

"If you think I am making fun, you are wrong," the sheriff said. "I see Anna Sarris is here, and Mikkel is waiting outside. Bring him in. He has always been a rascal—and you can't kill tough old men like him." The sheriff's voice had softened a little, and there was almost a smile on his face now.

Mikkel was brought in, still walking a little unsteadily as a result of his accident. But his eyes were as bright as ever, and he gave Johani and Anna a grin when he saw them.

"Stand with the other prisoners," the sheriff said sternly, and the grin left Mikkel's face.

After studying a paper in front of him for a moment or so, the sheriff looked up and said: "For stealing reindeer belonging to Jouni Sarris—eight hours' imprisonment. For assaulting a police officer guarding the same reindeer—eight hours' imprisonment. For hiding the Sarris herd and defying the police searchers—eight hours' imprisonment. What does that make?" He glared around the makeshift courtroom.

There was a bewildered silence. No one had expected Johani, Anna, and Mikkel to be punished.

"You aren't very clever," the sheriff grumbled. "Three eight-hour sentences make a full day. So you are all sentenced to one day's imprisonment—which you have served today," he said, smiling at his little joke. "That means you will be free, after you have dined with me. The court is over!" Stepping from behind the table, he walked across the room to pat Anna on the shoulder, and then he shook hands with Johani.

He gave old Mikkel a hard stare before asking, "What do the Sarris family pay you for being their herdsman? Much or little?"

Mikkel hesitated for a moment, and there was a roguish twinkle in his eyes when he replied, "They pay me enough."

The sheriff gave him a whack across the shoulders, then led the way into a side room where a meal had been prepared for them and Sergeant Peaksi. As the heaped plates of potatoes and boiled codfish were being laid on the table, the sheriff said, "I owe Sergeant Peaksi an explanation, and you owe him an apology." At the latter, he nodded to Johani and Anna. "I could not tell the sergeant that Niklander had confessed because we did not get the merchant's confession until just a few days ago. Before that, it was touch and go for a long while. So naturally Sergeant Peaksi still thought you were guilty of theft until he brought you in as prisoners."

"Mikkel and I are very sorry we had to treat the sergeant as we did," Johani admitted. "But we were desperate." He turned to Peaksi. "Sergeant, you must never pass the Sarris tent from now on without sitting at my mother's fire. There will be coffee and meat for you whenever you come. We shall never forget that you brought Mikkel back to life."

Sergeant Peaksi grinned. "Being a policeman among the Lapps teaches a man many things," he said quietly. "I never really thought you were thieves, but I had my duty to do. I admired your courage and determination, even though I had to be equally determined to arrest you."

"What I want to know," the sheriff said when the big platters had been cleared away and the last trace of cloudberry jam had disappeared, "is where you hid the herd. As you know, this wretched man Nillson complained to the Swedish government, and as a result we had to make special efforts to recover the reindeer—but it seemed that they had taken wings and flown to the North Pole."

"Can I say that we . . . just left them with a friend?" Johani asked. "The policemen did inspect that friend's tents, and saw his reindeer. But in winter everything is dark and ear-nicks are not easy to see, so the policemen

159

did not notice our herd had mingled with the reindeer of our friend."

The sheriff chuckled.

"I won't ask any more," he agreed. "And now I can tell you I have a surprise waiting. It isn't the Sarris herd which is going to vanish, but the Sarris family! A helicopter will be arriving soon to take you and your sister down to Rovaniemi. From there you will go by bus to the hospital. Tomorrow evening you should be with your father and mother. He has to stay in the hospital for a few more weeks, but otherwise he is completely recovered."

"And the herd?" Johani asked. "There are at least seventy-five new calves," he said proudly to Mikkel.

"When the Swedish Lapps bring it in," the sheriff said, "I am hoping that old Mikkel may be able to see to its needs—and at least prevent it from vanishing again. Now, we shall drink coffee, and then I must go. Lapps may be able to laze about, but we sheriffs are busy men." And he winked as he poured coffee for Anna.